AGAIN SANDERS

AGAIN SANDERS

EDGAR WALLACE

WILDSIDE PRESS

TO
LORD DEWAR

Originally published in 1928.

MAKARA, Chief of Kobala'ba, was paddled down the river to within ten miles of the residency and here he hired new paddlers from a lower-river village, leaving the ten girls who had paddled him so far in charge of the village headman.

He was young and skinny and beautiful to see, for not only did he wear the robe of monkey skins which is the robe of his rank, but his forearms were invisible under brass bangles; his hair was dyed red with ingola, his legs shone with oil, and he wore anklets of copper that clinked as he walked to the residency, where Mr. Sanders awaited him.

"I see you, lord Sandi," he greeted the Commissioner, and his voice had the quality of boredom and weariness.

"I see you, little chief," said Sanders, and there was acid in his tone. "And yet as I sat here before my fine house watching you come from the river, I had a strange thought. For it seemed to me that you were not Makara, son of Lebulana, son of Elibi that warrior, but a dancing woman of Kobala'ba, such as a man can buy for a thousand *matakos*."

If Makara felt shame he showed none.

"In my land all men are pretty," he said complacently. "Even in Kobala'ba I wear a feather in my hair and sometimes about my waist."

Sanders showed his teeth in a smile that was entirely mirthless.

"Rather would I see you with a spear in your hand and a shield on your arm, Makara," he said. "It seems that there are too many women in Kobala'ba——"

"Lord," said Makara eagerly, "that is why I came; for soon your lordship will send to us for the rubber and fish which you steal from us every year for your government, and because we are few men we have nothing to give."

Sanders took a cheroot from his pocket and lit it before he replied, his audience watching him anxiously.

"Was there tribute when I sent before?" asked Sanders. "And when I sent before then, did I find skins and rubber, and before then, even? Makara, your people of all the people on the river pay no tax to my king. And because you are far away and I cannot come in my little ship along the shallow river, I think you laugh at me. Strange stories come along the river to me—of women who hunt and women who fish, and women who build houses. It seems that there is a new race of slaves growing under my eyes: slaves who are penned like dogs and beaten like dogs. Which is against all the laws of all the tribes, but terribly against my law. Some day I will come and see."

"Lord, all that you hear is lies," said Makara, "for my young men are very strong and brave, and women have their proper place, which is in the fields and at the fires——"

"And at the paddles?" asked Sanders significantly. "My spies tell me that women brought you down the river, and that you left them at the village of Chubiri, so that I should not be offended. The palaver is finished."

Makara went back to his village a little uneasy.

For all that Sanders had heard was true: Makara had brought about a revolution in the custom of the country. In this black hinterland, men have a defined place and the sphere of their activities is rigidly confined by immemorial custom. For example, no woman is allowed to build a hut. The most lordly of the tribes reserve that work to men, partly, it is believed, because house-building has been the work of man since the beginning of time, and partly because, as is well known, a terrible curse lies on any roof that is thatched by a woman. No matter how indolent men may be, the erection of a house is their sole prerogative. On the other hand, no man with any spirit will till a field or grow corn or soak manioc or cook a meal. There once was a tribe so degraded that the men cooked their own dinners, and the name of that tribe was a reproach from the Lado to Eschowe. No woman may hunt or fish: that also is man's job, and the folk of Kobala'ba had terribly offended in this respect.

"They come by night from the little river between the grass," reported an indignant petty chief of the Isisi; "ten women in each canoe, and they spear fish under the eyes of my young men, and when my fishermen speak to them they answer them shamefully. Now, lord, because these are Akasava folk we can do nothing. A moon and a rime of a moon ago, I sent word to the great chief of the Akasava and told him of this terrible thing. He said that Kobala'ba was a country by itself, and that though the people were of his tribe they mocked him. Also, lord, they say that in Kobala'ba the women take their spears and hunt in the forest, and that the men sit at home in their huts, which is strange to me."

It is true that the village of Kobala'ba was sometimes called a country by itself, and with good reason. At the end of a shallow and narrow little creek which runs into the great river, and separated from all the world by a crescent of swamp, is a little lake on the northern shore of which rises a hog's back of good solid land. Here are long, sunny slopes where corn may be grown, and groves of Isisi palms affording pleasant shade, and behind the knoll a ten mile depth of forest, where men can hunt profitably, and women, too, as it seemed.

North of the creek is a girdle of swamp that separates the hunting ground from the forest of the Ochori; eastward is swamp again; to the west a desolation that is sometimes river and sometimes marsh. The isolation of Kobala'ba is complete. It is a dry oasis in a desert of water and near water, where crocodiles breed, and tiny mosquitoes rise in dense white clouds at every sunset.

In the days of the bad King Elibi, when his spears were triumphant from the Ghost Mountains to the Little River, Kobala'ba was uninhabited. Its inaccessibility, its isolation, the age-old legend of ghosts and devils, as many as the grasses that grew on its slope, made this place an undesirable residence. When Sanders broke Elibi in the early days of his mission, the remnants of an Akasava fighting regiment made its way to the little lake, taking the goats and wives it had acquired by violence. Here they established themselves in the huts they built, and

4

raised a new generation, which was mainly feminine—a phenomenon peculiar to the union of warriors and slaves. And that was the peculiarity of Kobala'ba, which persisted through the years, that three girls were born for every boy; so that in the course of time Kobala'ba was a village of straight-backed young women and puny youths who sat at the doors of their huts and were waited upon by sisters and cousins, mothers and aunts innumerable.

With the death of the old chief and the coming of Makara, a considerable change came over the economic life of Kobala'ba, and he discovered an easy way to wealth. Slavery became systematized; he sent out bands of women hunters, at first under the guidance of a man, eventually by themselves, and there accumulated in the village great stores of skins and rubber. His canoes brought him fish to be dried in the sun, and, with the skins and rubber, exported secretly across the frontier into the French territory.

Makara in another land might have become a captain of industry, for he was blessed with the gift of organization. Slavery is forbidden, but women have a price on the Great River, and it is lawful to buy wives. Makara and his enthusiastic men recruited a new kind of labour; his canoes went up and down the river seeking "wives." On the day he came to Sanders there were half a thousand women in his compounds and as many roving the forest in search of pelts.

At the end of three weeks' hard paddling, Makara's weary paddlers brought him to his village and to a domestic problem; for one of his wives, the tall T'lini, had led a band of huntresses into the forest and had returned almost empty-handed. Makara held a conference, which was attended by the forty-seven grown males of the village.

"We must not beat her or lay her in the sun," he said, "for presently Sandi will come, and she will tell evil stories about us. Let us be kind to her, and after Sandi is gone I will do certain things that will make her sorry."

T'lini, who had lain for twenty-four hours, her hands and feet tied together, in the big pen where the surplus women were kept, was released and well fed, and for seven days the male heads of families assembled their quotas and rehearsed them in the story they must tell. And it might well have been that the slave community would have grown undetected, and with it the wealth of Makara, had not science in two stout volumes come to Lieutenant Tibbetts of the King's Houssas.

Bones spent a fortnight of intensive reading and study before he started in to impart his newly acquired knowledge to the indigenous natives.

"What is it Bones is swotting so hard?" asked Sanders one night after Bones had made an unceremonious and hasty departure from the dinner table.

Hamilton knocked off the ash of his cheroot in his coffee cup, and his nose wrinkled disparagement.

"Science," he said laconically.

"Very admirable," murmured Sanders, and waited for the explosion, for Hamilton was on the touchy side, having just recovered from an attack of malaria.

"Science!" sneered Hamilton. "Astronomy, natural history, botany, biology. . . . My God, if he'd only keep it to himself!"

The two handsomely illustrated books which had come to Bones by the last mail dealt with science in a popular way, in all its aspects. The volumes had been edited by a great savant, the articles written by men with the gift of informing in the most simple language. Bones read and was fascinated. The two volumes exceeded in interest the modest expectations which were aroused by the sample page so cunningly dispatched to him.

"Science will have no mysteries for Bones," said Hamilton bitterly, "except perhaps the science of keeping the company accounts, and the science of doing a simple job without making a hash of it."

Sanders chuckled quietly.

"Bones must have spent a fortune on his correspondence lessons—but there's nothing selfish about him: he passes on all he learns."

"That's what I'm afraid of," said Hamilton darkly.

A fortnight after Bones had received these volumes of instruction, he gathered together the Houssas on the square, and with them their wives and families, and pointed to the star-encrusted sky, for it was a glorious night in early December—such a night as English astronomers dream about but never see.

"All people listen," said Bones in the Arabic of the Coast. "What are these little stars you see? Some are suns and some are worlds, greater than all this world——"

"Lord," interrupted a sergeant of Houssas respectfully, "if they be suns, why is it night, for all men know that when the sun shines it is daytime? Yet these little things shine only at night."

Bones explained laboriously, more or less inaccurately, and at the end violently.

Sergeant Abiboo reported the lecture to Hamilton.

"There is no doubt, Militini," he said, "that the lord Tibbetti is sick with the fever. For, as your lordship knows, when men are ill they imagine strange things, such as people walking about with heads like crocodiles."

"Why do you say this, Abiboo?" asked Hamilton.

"Because, lord," said the sergeant decisively, "Tibbetti told us that these stars are suns, when all men know they are stars, being the spirits of the dead, according to the Kaffirs, but, as we true believers know, the bright eyes of the blessed houris that look down from Paradise."

Bones, in disgust, turned from astronomy to biology. In consequence there was a marked coldness in the demeanour of the Houssas, and women scowled at him from their huts when he walked through the lines.

One Kano lady laid a complaint before Sanders.

"Tibbetti has shamed us all, for he told us that we were monkeys *cala cala*, and lived in trees and had tails; also that all men were once fishes, which is a terrible thing to say."

"The lord Tibbetti has made you a great riddle," said Sanders tactfully, "but because you are a stupid woman you cannot understand its mystery."

He passed a hint to Hamilton, and Hamilton, who never hinted, brought Bones to the carpet.

"You're demoralizing the detachment, Bones, with this pseudo-science of yours. Keep off biology and astronomy, and confine your lectures to metaphysics."

Bones brightened.

"Thank you, Hamilton, dear old officer. I don't know much about physics, but what about the odd spot of chemistry, dear old sir? Why does a seidlitz powder fizzle? You don't know, old boy! Don't pretend you do——"

"Metaphysics has nothing whatever to do with chemistry," said Hamilton coldly.

"Then," demanded the scornful Bones, "why call it physics—I ask you, dear old thing? Don't answer if you feel you're incriminating your jolly old self."

Bones was due for a trip to the Akasava. There were palavers to be held, a certain amount of taxation to be collected. More especially, Sanders wanted exact information as to what was happening at Kobala'ba.

The night before Mr. Tibbetts left on his journey, Hamilton uttered a word of warning.

"When you get to Makara's village don't be scientific—if you are, confine yourself to insects. You can't do any harm there. If you start working off little pieces about the universe to the bloodthirsty Akasava, you'll probably start a couple of wars. And I absolutely forbid you to talk about evolution. The Darwinian theory is distinctly unpopular amongst the Houssas. It may bring you into some disrepute with people who hunt monkeys and eat fish——"

"Tell them about bees, Bones," put in Sanders. "An object lesson in industry will do the Akasava no harm."

"A little astronomy, dear old Commissioner!" pleaded Bones. "What about the jolly old constellation of O'Brien? What about Beetlegrease, the notorious and ever famous star that's a hundred and fifty million times bigger than the sun?"

"Orion and Betelgeuse are the two words you're groping for," said Hamilton sternly, "and you'll not say a word about them. You remember the trouble we had with the Northern Ochori people over the moon, sir?"

Sanders nodded.

Long before Bones had taken science seriously, he had explained to the wild and terrified people of the Ochori the substance, character and origin of the lunar orb, with disastrous consequences; for the Northern Ochori, who blamed Bosambo for everything that had happened to the world since its beginning, gathered their spears and went up against their paramount chief. You cannot overturn settled convictions without producing unexpected reactions, and it took Sanders the greater part of a year to convince these misguided people that their first information about the moon was correct, namely, that it was the bright hole in the sky through which M'shimba-M'shamba made his entrances and exits from a disturbed and storm-swept earth.

Kobala'ba is not easily reached. The motor-launch dropped Bones at the scarcely visible mouth of the shallow river, and for four days he was paddled through bush and grass and virgin mosquito hordes—a painful experience.

He came to Kobala'ba in the dark of an evening; and, knowing him to be at hand, the villagers burnt a big bonfire on the beach, which served the double purpose of beacon and illumination.

It was not the chief Makara who met him, but T'lini, his wife, a very tall and supple girl of seventeen.

"Lord, I see you! I am T'lini, wife of Makara."

"I see you, T'lini," said Bones, peering at her. "Yet I think I would rather see the chief, your husband, for I do not make palaver with women."

He looked left and right along the crowded beach. Not a warrior was to be seen; only these straight, ebony figures regarding him gravely. She read his thoughts and said:

"There are few men in this village, lord Tibbetti, and these put themselves to bed early, because of the cold air of night which gives them pain in their throats."

Bones gaped at her.

"Good lord!" he said, in English.

"Also, lord," she went on quickly, "these women you see are the wives of our warriors, and they are so happy that they dance with joy because their men are kind. And every day we work in the fields whilst our husbands go hunting in the forest."

Bones screwed his monocle into his eye, and T'lini shrank back in terror.

"Tell me, T'lini, are you of this village?"

She nodded, which meant "No."

"I come from B'lini on the river. Makara bought me for a bag of salt, also my own sister and the daughter of my father."

Bones scratched his nose but said nothing. He walked to the hut that had been made for him. Here was a fine skin bed to spread his valise upon, and, rejecting the inevitable offer of service with the invariable excuse, he lay down and slept, for he was a very tired man.

It was dark when he woke: the phosphorescent dial of his watch told him it was within a quarter of an hour of dawn, and he rose and dressed. The place was already alive; fires were burning before each hut; shadowy figures flitted up and down the broad street; and with the first violent light of the sun he saw a small body of men coming down from the far end of the village, where Makara's hut was. Makara himself led the party, and very formidable it was, for each man carried a bunch of hunting spears, though the fineries which decked their persons seemed a little inappropriate.

"O Tibbetti, I see you!" boomed Makara. "Give me salt[A] if I did not come to you last night, but I and my young men, who have been hunting for many days in the forest, were tired. And to-day we go out on a long and terrible journey to find fish and rubber for Sandi and his king."

[A]

Salt—pardon.

8

"That is a good palaver," said Bones satirically, as he glared at the hunting party through his eyeglass.

With the exception of Makara, they were very fat young men, whose flabby flesh suggested anything but prolonged exercise.

"But first you shall tell me what place is this."

He pointed to a bare square of hard earth, where once a slave pen had stood —recently, he guessed. It had its fellow a few paces down the slope towards the river. His quick eyes detected a third and a fourth. Four big huts that had been recently demolished. There were others in all probability, if he looked for them.

Makara answered glibly enough, but his explanation was lame. Bones watched the hunters disappear through the thin woods that lead to the greater forest, and then he called an assembly of all the people, and went up to the palaver house, to find himself confronting a crowd of a thousand sober-faced women.

"O people," said Bones, "I have come a long way because my lord Sandi cannot make this journey to see you. By night and by day I have journeyed in my canoe along a terrible little river to take taxes for my king. And none are here. For the men who should be warriors and hunters are like children, and have grown lazy, so that there is no rubber or fish for my Government. Now I will tell you a story about bees that you may tell your children and your men."

Bones had an amazing vocabulary. They listened fascinated whilst he told the story of the economy of the hive. When he had finished, T'lini, who was squatting at the foot of the little hill, rose.

"Lord, that is a great riddle," she said. "Now tell me and my sisters: these little things who fly and do no work—are they men folk or women folk?"

"Men folk," said Bones, in an unguarded moment.

"And, lord, those who work and gather riches—what are they?"

Bones explained again; became a little inarticulate as they drew him out of his depth.

"That is a good tale," said T'lini, when he had finished. "Rubber we have got, and the skins of wild beasts, but we do not see these things again, and when we ask our lords they say that Sandi has come with his soldiers and taken them for his Government. Now tell us, lord Tibbetti, how may the women bees live through the cold, wet days, but do not the little things that fly and do no work eat up all the riches the women bees have gathered?"

Bones, sure of himself, explained.

"T'lini, that is a good question. Now I will tell you. They who do no work are killed when the wet days come, for the little women bees drive them from the nest and destroy them. And the next season come new little men and they last their season, and at the end are killed."

"Who rules this land of bees?" asked T'lini.

"One who is higher than any—a queen," said Bones, waxing poetical; "one who is as great as Sandi and wiser than I. And all the bee-women honour this one and bow their heads and clap their hands with joy whenever this high one walks abroad."

He saw nearly a thousand mouths opened in amazement and was gratified. Later that day he sent a messenger with a letter to Sanders.

"Dear Sir dear sir" (it ran rapidly)
   "Kobalarber is full of feamales feemailes femmales but the men have gone hunting I don't think I don't think."
   (Bones had this little trick of repetition.)
   "I talked about beas bes and how they worked in a scentifick sientifick manner. Femails deeply impresed. Shall stay the week am giving annother leckture on botny tomorow."

A month later he returned to headquarters.
"Did you give 'em any science?" asked Hamilton.
"Bee-ology, dear old sir—the habits and customs of the jolly old bumble, and a few words about the naughty old honey-maker, as per my letter of the 24th inst. The whole proceedings terminated with a vote of thanks to the chairman."
"Did you see Makara?" asked Sanders.
Bones smiled.
"Not too much, sir. I stayed in the village four days, and the naughty old deceiver and his boy friends didn't come back. They'd only gone about four miles into the forest."
He struck a more serious note when he told the results of his investigations.
"Slavery, eh? I was afraid so," said Sanders gravely. "An ingenious idea, and not the first time it has been practised in the Akasava country."
He sent for a carrier pigeon and, writing a message, flew the bird to one of his spies on the Upper River. Long before the order for Makara's arrest could be executed, there was an alarming outbreak of science at Kobala'ba.

• • • • •

A few nights after Bones' departure, Makara squatted by the fire of his hut, relating to certain close friends, counsellors and male sycophants, the details of a summary administration of justice. For he had taken T'lini his wife and had beaten her till he was tired, and she had run away into the forest to join a party of wives in their search for a peculiarly succulent monkey that was very satisfying to Makara's epicurean taste.
"She cried 'Wow!' and put her hands up," said Makara with relish. "Then she made a great noise and put her arms so . . ."
He stopped, peering up the village street towards the wood, where a small column had emerged from the trees—a column that must be made up of hunting parties that were not due for days, and should have been scattered through the hundred and fifty square miles of game preserves. They marched steadily, carrying neither monkeys nor skins, and there was something very peculiar about their solidarity. Ominous, too, for the red of the setting sun turned their spear-heads to the colour of blood.

"O woman," said Makara, in a passion, as T'lini approached him, "I will whip you——"

A spear-head dropped to his throat and pricked him sorely. He collapsed in a panic and was incapable of resistance, as two strong women bound him foot and hand. They laid the forty-seven males of Kobala'ba, fan fashion, about the palaver house, and T'lini, the chief's wife, spoke.

"Tibbetti, the son of Sandi, told us this tale," she said, looking down at the horrified face of her husband, who was the victim nearest to her. "*Cala cala* all the bee women worked and gathered their magic from flowers, and the bee men sat at home in their huts and ate all that was brought to them, and did no work and killed their wives. And then all the bee women held a palaver and they said: 'From this day we will kill the bee men at the end of every season, and in the next season we will get new men and kill them also when we are done with them.' And Tibbetti said that because of this great magic all the bee people are happy, so that you hear them singing as they go about their work. Tibbetti told us this, and he is wise, for he has three eyes and sees more than we."

She walked to the side of her husband and looked down at him, her spear poised.

"Now I think we shall be happy," she said, and struck as he had taught her. . . .

So slowly did news travel in that backwater of life that it was nearly a month before Sanders heard of the happening. It was brought by a lithe woman warrior who carried her spears with an air.

Sanders listened, and, seasoned as he was to strange happenings in this strangest of lands, the simple recital took his breath away.

"And now there are no men in Kobala'ba," concluded the messenger, "but next season we will go to the river villages and take such as we wish. But, Sandi, we wish for a ruler, and because we know you are kind to your people we have had a great palaver, and this is agreed, that we ask you, Sandi, to send us your son Tibbetti, that he may be our Queen Bee according to his magical words."

"Deuced awkward," said Bones dismally, as he pulled at his long nose.

THERE was a man of the Isisi whom all feared—even the very chief of that nation. He was no great warrior, nor was he skilled in magic. His name was M'anin and he was of the common people; a tall, thin man with a stammering voice, who did no more than talk. But his talk was very bitter and he respected nobody. Once, in the days of his beginnings, the chief of his village (afterwards chief of the tribe, and eventually hanged for the murder of a missionary) had taken a pliant *chicotte* and had gone in search of the talker. And M'anin had seen him coming and was panic-stricken, for he had spoken very evilly of this chief and certain of his wives. Yet, though his heart was like water, he met the chief with outward insolence, having in his soul the dim beginnings of a theory which happened to be right; and this theory was that he who talks and talks and supports one boldness with another may cow even the strongest and most enraged man or woman.

"I see you, chief," he greeted his furious master. "Oh ko! You are like a monkey that is caught by a spear! Now I must tell you the truth—you have a bad face and you are no proper chief for this village. And if Sandi knows this he will put you away."

So strong and bold were his words that the chief wilted before him.

"M'anin, have I spoken evilly of you? Have I done ill to you? And yet you make me foolish before my people."

M'anin looked at him thoughtfully.

"I speak truth, and if any man be hurt by truth that is his palaver. I speak as my mind is—even to Sandi."

He grew to maturity well hated but uninjured. Men, and women too, went out of their way to placate him; choice foods came to his house, lest the giver writhe under the lash of his criticism. Though the Isisi are river folk, and uncleanliness an abomination, none cavilled at M'anin, who never brought his body to the water. He dwelt apart with a fat woman, in shape like a beetle, and she was the audience on whom he practised when others failed. He neither hunted nor worked, and because he brought little to his own larder he was wont to sit at food with such families as advertised the excellence of their meals by the fragrance of their cooking pots. And none dared deny him for fear of his tongue.

And sometimes he would stand with his back to a tree, surrounded by young men, and talk of the badness of such things as were in their eyes good. In his eyes the wealthy Ogani, the hunter, and B'lini, whose canoes haunted the river, were an offence, and he reserved his bitterest gibes for those who had passed him in the race.

"Let all people look at Ogani, whom men call a great hunter. To me he is like a fish upon land, leaping here and there and opening and shutting his silly mouth. . . . Oh, people, why do you shiver at Sandi? For is he not a man with one life and can he eat two meals at once? He is no great ruler, for did not the crops fail?"

Sanders may have heard of this, but he was very lenient with talking men, and M'anin, satisfied with his daring, did not repeat his slander.

Then one fatal night somebody spoke of Bones. Now Lieutenant Tibbetts might be a figure of fun to his immediate associates. He was undoubtedly a rather impetuous young man, who both said and did irresponsible things. But to the people of the upper river Tibbetti was lank vengeance who had stalked evil men and had hanged chiefs without mercy; the memory of the staccato rattle of his machine-gun remained with certain tribes for a long time.

"This Tibbetti is no more than a fool," said M'anin. "Also he has no eyes, but puts a little glass where his eye should be."

"Oh ko, M'anin!" said one of his shocked hearers. "Did he not destroy the Leopards that crept into our huts at night and left us without faces?"

He spoke of that strange secret society which is known in one form or another from one end of Africa to the other.

"Oh ko!" mocked M'anin. "Did he not bring soldiers by tens and tens to do this little work? And are not the Leopards friends of the people?"

His words created a sensation. Never before had any man openly defended these terrible people. Intoxicated by his success, M'anin, who would as readily have championed the forces of the law, given sufficient provocation, went on:

"These Leopards are wonderful folk and have a great ju-ju. And to-day they live. I with my eyes have seen them. They are very kind to poor men and very hard to rich men. He who is a Leopard is great in the eyes of ghosts and it is said that M'shimba-M'shamba himself is their mighty spirit."

This was the beginning; the idle words of a talkative man bore fruit in the Isisi, but it was nipped in the blossoming stage by the chief of the Ochori.

By all standards wherewith despotic kings may be judged, Bosambo of the Ochori was a wise ruler. For he had the prime instinct of government—he knew to the second when he must give way and when he must stand, granite-like, be the prospect never so dark and the dangers appalling. He was not to be moved by such trifles as personal popularity or unpopularity, so that, when a small chief who was an admirer of M'anin made a bad song about Bosambo and likened him to a snake and a fish and a particularly comical ju-ju (one of those ju-jus of ancient times whose potency had atrophied) he sent no summons to the poet, nor did he visit upon him the weight of his anger.

Only in the days of the taxations, M'lipi, the chief in question, found that his contribution to the state was stolen en route to the Ochori city, and he had to levy yet another toll upon his cursing village.

And when his spies brought news of old men gathering secretly in the woods and speaking against him as an oppressor of the people (which he was not) and a rapacious foreigner (which he was), he said insulting things about the intelligence of old men and said no more. But when, in a quiet place, four men came together and said:

13

"These are the days of women—Wa! I have not drawn blood with my claws," and that speech was reported, Bosambo called his six best captains to him.

"In such a village are four men who are Leopards. Go swiftly and kill, but let no man see the killing."

And the captains went out by night and travelled till dawn, when they slept through the day. At night they moved again and by diligent enquiry found the spot where the new Leopards held a lodge.

They were talking over the matter of initiations when the six appeared with their shields on their arms and their killing spears in their hands.

"Come with us," said the chief of the six, and led them away to a deep ravine, and there they killed them, leaving what was to be left to the real leopards who live here in families.

Bosambo's great hut was on the river side of the city, and between his hut and the water were only his fields of corn and the huts of his guard. For a time might come when he would need the open space that led to where his three big canoes were ranged on the beach.

Here, in huts so near to the river that you might fish from them, dwelt the young men who were spearmen or paddlers as occasion demanded. They were tall, straight young men, very strong and terribly brave, and very proud, for each man wore a scarlet cotton handkerchief bound about his head which was the livery of the king.

Bosambo sat in the shade of a large grass mat one sweltering day, speaking to the chief of his guard, Bosongo, and the talk was of a woman of the Isisi. None of his intimate guard was married; marriage meant retirement to the mass which did not wear handkerchiefs about their heads.

"Lord Bosambo, I think my time is come, for this woman is very wonderful to me and her father is rich. I will build a hut and be your man and you will make me the head of a fighting regiment, as you made T'furi and M'suri Balana and other men."

Bosambo pulled steadily at his long-stemmed pipe and obscured the still air with a cloud of rank-smelling smoke.

"This I will do, Bosongo, but the Isisi are a strange folk and will not let their women cross the river to live in a strange land. Now here in the Ochori are women in plenty."

Bosongo nodded, which meant his disagreement.

"This girl is strong for me, and when her father has given me the salt and rods and goats which come with her, I will bring her by night in a canoe to this land and that will be the end."

But Bosambo was not so easily convinced. A breach or two of national custom meant little to him, but here was a possibility of trouble, for the Isisi at this moment was in its most truculent mood. The harvest had been good, men were rich in corn and salt, and in such circumstances the risk of war was great.

"If there is a killing palaver what may I say to my lord Sandi, who is almost my brother? For did we not go to the same mission school and learn of Marki,

Luki and Johnni which are white men's mysteries? I will think of this, Bosongo, and in one day and two days I will tell you what is in my mind."

"Lord," said Bosongo eagerly, "there will be no bad palaver; for this woman has often come to my house with her father and his paddlers."

Bosambo stared at him blankly.

"I have seen no little chief of the Isisi in this city," he said.

Bosongo grew uncomfortable.

"He brought her by night, knowing how I love this woman. In the morning he took her away."

Bosambo said nothing more, but with a lordly wave of his hand dismissed his guard.

That evening between the lights came a spy of his from the Isisi, for Bosambo took no chances. The Leopardism which four machine-guns and a company of Houssas had stamped out three years before was rampant again from the Lower Akasava to the Upper Isisi, though the rope that hanged the chief of the Leopards still swung its ravelled strands in the breeze.

For an hour they sat in conference in the dark of his hut, the spy and the chief of the Ochori. Then in the darkness the spy crept away, followed the river's course for a mile till he came to a canoe with five paddlers, and in the bottom of the canoe a man bound with native rope and gagged uncomfortably. He spoke a few words and, stooping, the paddlers lifted their prisoner from the bottom of the canoe, stayed long enough to pull the boat high and dry before they cut the bonds of the man's feet and took the gag out of his mouth.

"Walk with me, little Leopard," said the spy.

They gave the man a drink of water.

"If you speak what is true to Bosambo he will do you no hurt," they told him, and with this assurance he walked silently in their midst until they came to the edge of the Ochori city, through which they led him by back ways to Bosambo's great hut, where it was his practice to sleep alone.

And there he talked and talked and talked, being rendered the more loquacious by large draughts of native beer. In the end Bosambo was well satisfied.

That night came three Isisi leopards who had learnt in some mysterious way of the killings in the ravine. They came noiselessly in one black canoe, and, threading their way between the habitations of his guard, came to the king's hut. And on their hands were gloves of leopard pads with ripping steel claws, which is the insignia of the society. One wormed his way into Bosambo's hut and struck with the knife he carried, and when he felt the body shudder, he used his clawed pad as the ritual directed. . . .

The murderer was crawling to the door when a huge hand gripped his neck and thrust his face downward, in another second a knee was in the small of his back. He tried to fight up, but only for a second. A short club of dried rubber struck him. When he recovered consciousness he was sitting with his back against a tree; the ghastly glow of dawn was in the sky, and even as he blinked from left to right the sun was up.

"O man, I see you," said Bosambo. "Behold this evil thing which you have done!"

He looked to the right and the prisoner's eyes followed. He saw the captured Leopard lying stark and awful to see. The two paddlers who had accompanied him he did not see, for they were dead in the river.

"This man you have killed, therefore you go to Sandi for his judgment," said Bosambo virtuously; "for I cannot kill you because I have spoken my word, and in the country where I govern for Sandi and his king no man breaks the law. But first you will tell me who sent you, also who is the new chief of your Leopards and many other interesting and beautiful things."

The prisoner glared at him.

"The Leopard hates and dies," he said conventionally. "Well you know, Bosambo, that we Leopards do not speak of our dreadful ju-ju."

"You shall speak to me," said Bosambo, "and if you hate, then by Ewa! which is death, you shall hate me worse before you die at the end of Sandi's long rope, with all his soldiers mocking at you."

An hour later he squatted down at a box and began a laborious epistle, all the more laborious because he wrote on that which was as thin as cigarette-paper, using a pen. When he had finished, the pigeon was waiting, and the message was bound about one red leg.

"Go swiftly, little friend of soldiers," said Bosambo, and flung the bird high.

• • • • • •

At Houssa headquarters was a very irascible Chief Staff Officer, who hated Lieutenant Tibbetts with a hatred beyond understanding—unless you allowed for the fact that he drank too much and suffered from a complication of tropical diseases all of which were disturbing to a man's temper in a country where 102 in the shade is considered fairly cool.

His name was Omes, and the words of Omes, written and spoken, were calculated to disturb even the serenity of a young man so perfectly balanced and so completely lost to a sense of inferiority as Bones.

They met once when Major Omes was on a tour of inspection.

"Very nice, very nice indeed!" he said after inspecting company accounts. "I suppose you are the officer responsible?"

"Yes, sir," said Bones, purring.

"It was not done by an il-lit-er-ate savage who had recently learnt the ru-di-ments of the English lang-uage?"

He spoke like that.

"No, sir," said Bones.

"You will pardon my error," said Major Omes sweetly, "but ex-am-ining these accounts, in-de-cipherable as they are, my mistake is nat-ural. Never in my life have I seen such a horror!"

And so on. He wrote in the same strain—and wrote weekly.

16

Bones had passed a restless month in the pursuit of knowledge and the forgetfulness of certain unpleasantnesses. It was by no means a quiet pursuit. When Bones was intensely interested in a subject, he employed quite a lot of his waking or talking moments, the terms being synonymous, in an endeavour to work up his unfortunate friend to an interest of the same intensity.

It was not a correspondence course on which he was engaged; somebody had sent him a book on "Transmigration." It must have been written originally for children, for he understood every argument.

The passing on usually began at breakfast, and Hamilton, who recognized the symptoms, would make a fine effort to head off the student to the contemplation of sordid and mundane things.

"Do you realize, dear old sir," began Bones, on this morning, "that the soul, bein', as it were, a jolly old transient, that is to say a thing that is always poppin' off here an' there——"

"Will you kindly pop off to the clothing store after breakfast and count the trousers-short-drill?" asked Hamilton. "And when you've finished popping there, will you pop over to the company office and check the medical history sheets of the detachment? Major Omes has written."

"Certainly, dear old Ham. But leave old Omes out of it, old boy—why make me sick, dear old emetic?" said Bones. "What I mean to say is, dear old sir, do you realise that your soul was once in a duck, old boy—or maybe a snake, old officer? Perfectly ghastly, isn't it? On the other hand, dear old Ham, how well you've got on! It's quite possible, Ham, that once you were just a jolly old cat! I might have been hoofin' you off the verandah for pinchin' the chop!"

"You were most certainly a laughing jackass," growled Hamilton, "or a parrot."

"Bird of Paradise, dear old soul," said Bones instantly. "It's rum, Ham, but I've often dreamt I was flyin' with feathers stickin' out of my jolly old nut."

"That was when you were an angel, you silly goop," growled Hamilton.

"My point is——"

"Oh, *do* shut up, Bones!" groaned Sanders.

Bones bowed.

"I wouldn't object," said Hamilton later, when he and Sanders were alone, "but as usual he is demoralizing the detachment. Abiboo, who is a strict Mussulman, got up in the air because Bones suggested he might have been once a guinea-pig."

But Mr. Tibbetts' obsession did not end with the suggestion that he had met his companions in other incarnations. His own reminiscences were a little trying.

"I had it this mornin', old boy," he said to Hamilton. "Just a flash, dear old officer; it all came back. Rome, dear old Nero, the Hippodrome where the poor old johnnies were being burnt to death—everything."

"Where you Nero or the Hippodrome?" asked Hamilton wearily. "I suppose you really mean the Coliseum?"

"One of those halls, Ham. There was Nero sittin' in a stage box all gold an' purple; there was me——"

"In the orchestra?" suggested his bored friend.

"No, Ham—in the pit, bein' chased by lions all over the beastly ring. I sort of felt his naughty old nose on my shoulder an' he was just goin' to grab me when I came to myself."

"Pity," said Hamilton. "If you'd only waited a second I should be applying for a new subaltern."

Bones shrugged his shoulders and went back to his hut to finish a letter which he had begun and which was addressed to *The New Incarnation: a Journal of Consciousness*.

The hobbies of Bones would have been fairly unimportant but for this illusion of his, that every new idea which struck him was something well worth imparting to others.

Then came the pigeon with Bosambo's warning in scrawled Arabic. Sanders read and was troubled. He had that uncanny instinct for first causes, and for an hour he pondered the dramatic reappearance of the Leopards and found at the end a satisfactory explanation.

He sent for Bones, and to his astonishment Mr. Tibbetts came, holding a fluttering telegraph form in his hand, and on his face a most woebegone expression.

"What's the trouble?" asked Hamilton. "Has dear old Omes——"

"Popped off, old boy," said Bones dismally. "Gathered to his dear old papas. Fearfully bad luck."

"Omes?" asked Hamilton, raising his eyebrows incredulously.

"Jolly old angel," said the gloomy Bones, "practically speaking. I've never been so fearfully upset in all my life."

"Dead?" asked Hamilton.

"Almost, old boy. Collapsed—rushed him on the steamer. Terrible old wreck."

Major Omes had indeed all but gone the way of humanity. Following a heavy night at mess, and a hot morning, and a misguided attempt to reduce his obesity with a new and patent apparatus, there almost occurred a vacancy in the Army List.

"Very bad luck," said Sanders, who in such moments as these was no sentimentalist. "But I want you to take twenty men and a machine-gun into the Isisi country, arrest M'anin and bring him to headquarters. Arrest also Tigisaki and B'welo. . . ."

He named half-a-dozen names.

"And if they oppose, shoot. The Leopard is putting his head up. This time bring back the whole skin."

Bones left in the *Zaire*, and for the time being forgot his studies. There was excuse for his forgetfulness; for ten days he chased Tigisaki and his ten novitiates through the swamps to the edge of the Old Man's Country. Another week he spent prying into strange rites which had been performed in the sickle light of the moon. It was a ghastly business, involved certain unpleasant diggings, but in the end the Leopard's claws were drawn and Bones and his twenty soldiers ploughed through the forest to the Isisi city, and there he sat in judgment in the little palaver house on the verge of the river.

M'anin came, full of faith in his magical conversation, though he stood between two Houssas with fixed bayonets.

"I see you, Tibbetti," he said, with easy insolence. "Now I will tell you truly, for in the full of the moon there came a new strong spirit into me, and it seemed that the soul of a strong white man had come to my heart."

"Eh?" said Bones, who was instantly the student of psychology. It was in the full of the moon that the truculent Major Omes had been struck down in his pride.

"That is what my heart felt," said M'anin; "and I can speak to you without fear, for you are only a small man and very foolish. You are like a child, and men laugh at you. I have seen none so like the little monkey who sits on the trees."

Bones listened agape, and, satisfied with the impression he had made, M'anin the talker went on.

"Now you shall leave me and these people and go away," he said; "and I will bring the Leopards back. For did I not raise them up when they were dead, and teach them to go into the forest with claws, and sit while they danced and made their magic? This I tell you because I do not fear you. You are like a fish——"

Suddenly Bones' accusative finger shot out.

"Omes, dear old boy," he squeaked in English, "you've got into the wrong body—and you're for it!"

He turned to Sergeant Abiboo.

"O man, put a rope on that tree," he said.

THY NEIGHBOUR AS THYSELF

THERE was once an earnest administrator who brought to the control of all the territories a sense of order which was almost devastating in its thoroughness.

He discovered, as so many men new from armchairs in Whitehall have discovered, that (to quote his own report):

> "The laws of the native territories are in a condition of chaos. In some areas tribal customs are accepted by responsible officials as adequate substitutions of the law. In other areas, there has come to be observed a compromise between the laws sanctioned by the Imperial Government and laws which apparently are based upon the primitive reasonings of the native tribes and peoples. . . ."

He set himself to rectify this undesirable state of affairs, and in four years produced a compromise of his own which is still known as the "Little Tich Code" wherever hot and sarcastic magistrates, commissioners and commanders of troops meet to discuss their morning peg.

There were many objectionable customs practised in the territory controlled by Mr. Commissioner Sanders. Given an expeditionary force, the liberal employment of machine-guns and a couple of years of martial subjugation, these habits of the people would (possibly) be eradicated.

Behind Sanders in his more drastic treatment of native misbehaviour was the implied sanction of the people he punished. He stamped out the general practice of witchcraft and human sacrifice, he discouraged with rope and irons the formation of secret societies, he dealt hardly with raiders, but he walked warily when he had to deal with customs which were logically sound, however revolting they might be in the eyes of civilized Europe.

And, peculiarly enough, one of the most revolting of these found favour in the eyes of the busy administrator, as he stated, in an article brightly intituled *Notes and Observations on Primitive Customs*, and published in a magazine which is only to be seen in the reading rooms of ancient clubs and the waiting rooms of modern dentists.

One day (long after the administrator had been replaced) there came a letter to headquarters. It was addressed to "The Officer, Controller or Commissioner in charge."

Lieutenant Tibbetts occupied that responsible position, for Sanders was in the Isisi on a tour of inspection, and Captain Hamilton had gone a three-day journey into the bush to shoot leopards.

Bones opened the letter and discovered that it was intended for him. How otherwise could he regard a document which began:

"Sir,"

"I am addressing this in the faint hope that it may fall into the hands of an official with the glimmerings of scientific knowledge. It matters not to me what rank you be, sir, provided you are intelligent, alert to the decadence of the age and the effete tendencies of so-called civilization. . . ."

Bones answered the letter, and there began a correspondence which continued for the greater part of a year.

Nobody really bothered their heads about Bones and his correspondence. Sanders observed that from time to time weighty volumes appeared from their wrappings. Hamilton noticed the growing studiousness of his subordinate.

"Taking a correspondence course, Bones?"

"No, sir," very gravely.

"How to learn the saxophone in three lessons?"

Bones smiled pityingly.

"Or is it 'Every man his own lawyer'?"

Bones shrugged.

"Dear old officer, why burble, dear old sir? Why blither? Bad symptom, Ham, old boy—fearfully bad. It shows the epiglostium's all wrong, old officer; your medella's not functioning, old Ham!"

When he had gone back to his hut:

"Bones is taking some sort of medical course," said Sanders. "By the last mail he had a book on Eugenics."

Hamilton was not absolutely sure what eugenics were: he tackled his subordinate on the subject.

"You wouldn't understand it, Ham," said Bones gently. "It's all about your jolly old body—not yours, old boy, but anybody's."

"Is it something to do with patent medicines?" asked Hamilton suspiciously.

Bones' smile was very superior.

Hamilton was impressed, a week later, to learn that Bones' correspondent was no less a man that Sir Septimus Neighbour. Even he had heard of Sir Septimus. He lived in Harley Street, where he had for many years been the highest paid and the most famous of consultants. He was the author of innumerable works on Eugenics, and was the founder of the back to nature movement which had once brought him into conflict with the police. Had he not led a procession of semi-nudities into Hyde Park to protest against the unhygienic character of modern dress? Then he carried his theories into practice, adopted for house wear a pair of shorts and sandals. That his servants should give him notice was inevitable; that dowagers should sway and all but swoon when, calling to discuss growing adiposities, they were confronted by an encouragingly thin gentleman in running shorts and sandals. His consulting practice fell away. He became (as he said) a victim of medical persecution, and, having money and leisure, he plunged deep into a sea of newspaper controversy and thoroughly enjoyed himself.

And then Bones began to give up wearing clothes. He discarded socks and puttees and appeared one morning at breakfast in his bare, thin legs. Hamilton shuddered but did not protest. A few days later Bones came to lunch self-consciously in a sleeveless and diaphanous singlet. These, with shorts, constituted his entire raiment.

"Go back to your quarters and put on a pinafore!" snarled Hamilton.

"Hyjenny, old boy," murmured Bones.

Sanders said nothing.

It was rumoured from the Houssa lines that Bones even discarded the singlet and had been seen on the beach clad in a sun helmet and a palm fan. He did not deny this.

"Too many clothes, old officer," he said. "Back to nature—never felt better in my life. There's death in the pants, dear old sir—positively!"

He did not come to dinner that night. Hamilton went over to discover the reason, and found Bones' servant annointing his blistered back with cold cream.

"Got to get used to it, old boy—temp'ry incapacity . . . ultra purple ray, old officer—ouch! Oh, clumsy pig! Go easy with your big hands, for they are like N'gombi canoes!"

This latter in Coast Arabic to the annointing servant.

Subsequently Bones admitted the identity of his correspondent, and even Hamilton was impressed.

"He's coming out," said Bones, complacently.

"Here?" Hamilton looked incredulous.

"He's coming here," said Bones, and added: "On my invitation."

"Did he by any chance go through the formality of asking the invitation of the Secretary of State for the Colonies?" asked Hamilton coldly. "I realize that he's nobody in particular, but did you persuade him to get your invitation countersigned by that unimportant official?"

"Everything's in order, dear old officer." He looked thoughtfully at Hamilton. "Old boy, you're wearing too many clothes."

Bones himself was in his singlet, slightly humped on the back, where cotton wool protected his sun-blistered vertebræ.

"The old Neighbour says that the only people who understand life are the jolly old indigenous natives. He's going to live with 'em for a year."

"Does he speak the language, Bones?" asked Sanders, and to his surprise Bones nodded.

It was not surprising that Sir Septimus Neighbour should speak the language: he was the sort of man who held by Socrates and his incursions into Greek study at the age of eighty—or was it ninety? He had an extraordinary facility for acquiring strange tongues, and in six months knew more of the Bomongo tongue than the missionary (home on leave) who taught him.

Sanders fingered his chin thoughtfully. He did not like experiments; liked them less when they were carried out by men and women strange to the land.

The next mail brought a letter from Downing Street, which commended to his care the body and soul of Sir Septimus Neighbour, K.B.E., M.D., F.R.C.S., and the next boat brought the redoubtable specialist himself. He was a small man, painfully thin and bald; an irregular greying beard was a decoration to a face which badly needed assistance. He wore large horn-rimmed spectacles, and his baggage consisted of one suitcase, a butterfly net and a pair of rubber boots which were strapped on the outside of the case. His shorts were the shortest shorts Sanders had ever seen. From the waist upward he was bare, but he hid his boniness under a light drill jacket, a fact for which he apologized.

"I had some trouble on the ship, Mr. Sanders."

He had a high, shrill voice, and a range of restless gestures which were rather fascinating to watch.

"Prudes, my dear fellow, prudes! These European women are simply terrible."

Sanders glanced at Bones, who had gone down to meet the scientist. He, too, was self-consciously bare to the waist; his jacket pocket bulged—the Commissioner guessed that the singlet had been removed at the last moment.

"The people at home wish me to send you to one of the most primitive of our tribes," said Sanders, "and I have sent word to prepare a hut for you in the Lulanga district. They are so near to nature"—he concealed a smile—"that even the N'gombi regard them as a little indelicate."

Sir Septimus did not see the sarcasm. He inclined his head gravely.

"I could wish nothing better," he said. "As to the hut"—he shook his head. "I have done with huts and houses, flats and mansions. Under the bare sky, sir; on good old mother earth, sir. I wish to live as they live."

"They live in huts," said Sanders.

"I shall teach them to sleep in the open—that is my mission," said Sir Septimus with the greatest gravity. "I shall teach them the same example as my dear young disciple here has taught them." He waved his hand at the blushing Bones. "He tells me that he also sleeps on the bare earth, with a berry or two for breakfast, a little raw fruit for luncheon——"

"I've often done it," said Bones loudly. "I really and truly have, dear old Excellency! Ham, old boy, you'll bear me out: nature has always been my long suit, old officer."

"The last time you went up river," said Hamilton slowly, "you complained that there was too much ventilation in the sleeping cabin of the *Wigle* , and that the mattress wanted remaking. I seem to remember some little trouble about your sleeping bag going astray——."

But Bones had already taken Sir Septimus by the arm and had led him out on to the verandah. Later they were seen walking on the beach together.

"If they'd only worn bathing dresses I wouldn't have minded," said Hamilton, in despair. "You've no idea what Bones looked like. . . ."

He went into gruesome details.

On the following Sunday morning Sir Septimus left by canoe for the Lulanga, and only waited till he was out of sight of the residency before he took off the jacket which was his total concession to a hated civilization.

The province of Lulanga is sited at the narrowest part of the Opori River, a tortuously winding stream that runs into the forest and remains forest-fringed until it runs into the French territory.

The wisdom and primitiveness of the Lulanga folk were a tradition. Up and down the river it was known that since time began the Lulanga people had been wise in all their ways and crude in their habits of life. They were a branch of the Isisi family, yet owed and paid no allegiance to the King of the Isisi. They might be called (and were so called) N'gombi, which means no more than "dwellers in the forest," yet they were distinctly riverain folk and swam and fished from their childhood.

Bosambo, no stickler for inherent sovereignty, claimed them for Ochori and sent his captains to gather tribute. They paid without protest, but at the next grand palaver of chiefs over which Sanders presided, Bosambo made restitution and humbled himself.

For the wisdom of the Lulanga folk lay in this, that they saw to-morrow and knew that there were other days beyond, and their primitiveness was expressed in their adherence to old customs and the most ancient costume of all.

In all the world there are only three people who wear no clothes, and the Lulanga was one of them. You must remember that they persevered in this old practice in the face of the severest condemnation. There had been, in the past, wars waged by their cannibal neighbours to enforce upon them at least a homely loincloth; for the cannibal tribes of Africa are peculiar in this, that they are innately modest. But by their wisdom and their skill they had defeated their enemies and retained their simple privilege.

Sanders had argued with them and threatened them, but all to no purpose. He was successful in a more reprehensible practice, as old as the other. The Lulangas were the last tribe on the river to forgo with some reluctance the practice of slaying their stupid and their old. When a man or woman fell ill or met with some accident which permanently maimed them, or went mad as people do in a land where sleeping sickness is as common as a cold in England, then was S'boro called to their aid. S'boro was a mystic devil who only became potent if you boiled together three varieties of poison flowers and made from them, with a little manioc, a thin red paste. This was laid on the lips of the sick, the old, the mad and the feeble, usually whilst they were asleep, and in the morning they were dead enough to be buried.

The author of the "Little Tich Code" had in his article praised this practice—the praise cost him his job and earned the wrath and execration of Sanders, who had taken four years to eradicate the practice and then had only succeeded by a few judicious hangings. It pained him to punish so gentle and wise a people, but only through punishment could the practice be arrested. S'boro was no longer laid on sleeping lips, and in the Lulanga country there were quite a number of silly old people and crippled men, an offence to the fastidious and the cause of an undercurrent of discontent which Sanders did not even suspect.

Sir Septimus arrived on the ninth day of his journey, and the wise chief M'bongo and his eight headmen came down the narrow river to meet him and escort him to the chief's village. And here in the light of bonfires he landed in the dark of night, and saw girls with the figures of Venus and the faces of Gorgons

24

dance for him, and the chief gave him raw meal as a sign of his love, and led him to the hut that had been prepared for him. This shelter was loftily declined.

"O Chief," said Septimus, in his best Bomongo (by this time he was as near to nature as any man who wore only sandals and a helmet could be), "I sleep on the ground, for that is my mystery."

The wise chief told him of what happened to people who slept on the ground, and Sir Septimus changed his mind.

That night there was a long palaver, the chief and he sitting side by side, clasping their bare knees before the fire, which was uncomfortably hot.

"Sanders we love, because if we did not love him he would beat us," said M'bongo, with simple *naïveté*, "but he has taken away from us many of our ancient rules. Also he desired us to cover our bodies like the common people of the Isisi, but this we would not do because our fathers before us, and their fathers, did not cover their bodies, and were strong and beautiful. Also he said those who suffer may not go to sleep, because it was against the white man's law. And lord, who are a friend of Sandi and are wiser than all the world, you will know how bad it is for a nation that the old ones who can no longer work, and the mad who may bring into the world other mad ones, should live as we live. Up and down this river, amongst the Isisi and the N'gombi, and even the Ochori who are slaves, and the Akasava, this was the rule of the land till Sandi came, that those who could not work should die."

Sir Septimus nodded.

"That is a good palaver," he said.

M'bongo stared at him in astonishment and rising hope.

"Lord, that is very fine talk," he said, "and my people will be very happy."

Thus launched upon his favourite topic, Sir Septimus Neighbour, K.B.E., etc., expanded into oratory. What he said now he had said in his club a score of times to an admiring smoking-room audience.

"My dear fellow, what is the use of keeping the old and the sick? This country is going to the dogs. Wouldn't it be better to let them pass quietly away? Why let 'em live and be a misery, my dear friend? It's misery to themselves, my dear fellow. It's inhuman, it's unhygienic, it's against all the laws of nature. . . ."

In the more sonorous terminology of the Bomongo tongue he said very much the same thing and the wise chief M'bongo and his elders listened.

A month later one of Sanders' spies came unobtrusively to the Lulanga and rested a few days, watched and noted; on the fifth night he went swiftly down the little river to the master spy of the area, to whom he gave the news. It came eventually to Sanders when he was smoking an after-dinner cigar, and the Commissioner was worried.

"Bones' pal is doing a little cock-eyed propaganda work," he said. "It doesn't seem possible, but he appears to be undoing all my work in the Lulanga, and possibly on the river. Once S'boro gets busy again, the practice will hardly be confined to the Lulanga."

"What's the trouble?" asked Hamilton, waking up with a start, and Sanders told him.

"In the first place," he said, "this old crank has enrolled himself a member of the Lulanga nation, and insists upon being treated as a member of the tribe and on going out to work in the fields—that won't do him any harm. But what will do him and all of us a tremendous mischief is the eugenic doctrines he is teaching."

He told Hamilton of the theory which the old man was propounding.

Bones, who had grown a little weary of the back to nature movement and had gone to bed early that night in his famous striped silk pyjamas, was awakened by his superior an hour later.

"Sanders wants you to take the *Wigk* up river to the Lulanga, dig out old man Neighbour and bring him back to headquarters."

Bones sat up in bed, blinking uncomprehendingly and after Hamilton had repeated the message four times, each time with more violence, he understood.

"Dear old Sep," he said, "silly old ass. At the same time, Ham, old boy, there's a lot to be said for Sep. The old thing's perfectly right in theory. The survival of the fittest, as jolly old Shakespeare said——"

"Don't give me any lip," said Hamilton coarsely. "Hustle your crew and be ready to start at daybreak."

Bones rose wearily from his couch and went in search of Yoka, the steersman, B'fuli, the assistant engineer, and the six men who formed the nominal crew of the *Wigk* . To these he added six soldiers. He came at five o'clock in the morning to take coffee with Sanders and Hamilton, and he was in a five o'clock in the morning mood.

"It's fearfully inconvenient, dear old Ham, getting away without any preparations, wicked old sportsman. That beastly mattress is still full of bumps——"

"Whenever you feel sleepy," said Hamilton coldly, "draw up to the nearest bank, eat a couple of berries and go to sleep in a puddle—be natural, Bones!"

It was an hour after daybreak before the *Wigk* was ready to begin her voyage, and in that hour a pigeon arrived at headquarters with news which resulted in the doubling of the military escort. S'boro was active again, not only in the Lulanga, but there had been cases in the fringing villages of the Isisi. Old men and women had vanished; a woodman on whom a tree had fallen had died of some other cause than his injuries. There was a tag to the message, which came wrapped round the pigeon's red leg:

"Also the naked lord is ill, having eaten certain fruit which gave him great pains in the belly."

Bones' voyage was not a propitious one. He struck a sandbank that afternoon and was left high and dry in the middle of the river till the following morning, when sufficient natives could be summoned to push the *Wigk* into deep water. The chapter of accidents, thus begun, continued. He hit a submerged log on the second day, opened the tiny forehold of the boat, which sank by the head. She had to be beached with some haste and the hole filled with cement. She was not an hour from the beach when she went broadside on to yet another sandbank, and when she was got off it was found that the cement plug was shifted, and she had to be beached again.

Bones perspired and swore, but his accident was not without value. While he was waiting for more thorough repair at the hands of native Isisi workmen he learnt of a case of S'boro twenty miles in the forest, and with a dozen soldiers he made a forced march and came upon the village in time to interrupt the burial of two old men who had conveniently died the night before.

Now the Isisi are not as wise as the Lulanga people, nor are they quite as refined in their methods, and the evidence of violent death was here apparent. Bones acted promptly. He left the two murderers of the old men hanging from one branch of a tree, and brought back the headman of the village with irons on his wrist.

"Lord," said this man in an aggrieved tone, "I have done no harm, for the word has gone up and down the river that Sandi is strong for S'boro and has sent a wise old man to the Lulanga people to teach them new ways by which the useless folk may be put away. What shall we simple people believe, Tibbetti? Tell me that."

Bones turned on him with a mirthless and terrifying smile.

"O man," he said softly, "believe the two dead ones I left with ropes round their necks, for they speak so plainly of what my lord Sandi desires, that even the Isisi can understand!"

Two days passed before he came in sight of the beach. There was M'bongo, the wise chief, waiting for him, and all his councillors about him. Bones did not wait for the customary greeting, as his foot touched the shore he said:

"Chief, there is S'boro in this land, and I am come from Sandi to punish those who kill. Certain men who are old and mad have died in your village." He named them one by one.

He saw the chief's face fall. For a while he was silent, and then:

"B'rolu taught us this."

Now "B'rolu" is the name for "Neighbour." Bones was to discover that this was the native title that Sir Septimus had chosen.

"This great wise man is one of our people," said M'bongo proudly. "He walks with us like a common man and wears no clothes on his body, and he works in the field and makes straw mats."

"Where is he?" asked Bones.

He saw the chief's expression change.

"Lord, I think he is a little mad. He is in his hut and will not come out, and when we go to him we cannot get in because of the things he has placed in the doorway."

He led the way. On the outskirts of the village was a brand new hut. The door was blocked with branches of trees and billets of wood which had been hastily gathered in the night by Sir Septimus.

"O B'rolu!" called the chief.

A shrill voice spoke from the interior of the hut, and it spoke in English.

"Go away, you blackguard! Don't you dare come in here! Send for Mr. Sanders at once. By gad, I'll have you locked up!"

"Are you there, Sir Septimus?" said Bones anxiously.

"Who is it?" demanded the voice.

Bones had a glimpse of a wild eye staring through the interstices of the wood.

"Oh, it's you, you young jackanapes. What the devil do you mean by getting me up here? Have you any soldiers? I want that man hanged at once. The murderous blackguard. . ."

After some time the entrance of the hut was cleared and Sir Septimus emerged. He was very white and very shaky, and round his bare shoulders was a skin rug.

"Thank God you've come!" he quavered. "I've lived in terror for a week. I fell ill, and some of these beastly fellows came in and tried to put some stuff on my lips. I had to fight like the devil . . . the barbarous brutes!"

"Lord," pleaded M'bongo, when Bones had translated the complaint, "this great man asked us to treat him as though he was one of ourselves. It is true that one of my young men took S'boro to him, believing he was in pain, but this he also taught us to do."

· · · · ·

Bones went down to the beach to see Sir Septimus get on board the surf boat that was to carry him to the homeward-bound liner, and Bones was a little over-dressed if anything.

"Sorry you've had such a bad time, sir," he said, a little stiffly, "but this back to nature stuff is—er—well, dear old Sep. I ask you!"

Sir Septimus regarded him with a jaundiced eye.

"The whole country is rotten," he snapped, "everything . . . unhygienic . . . I shall have a few words to say to the Secretary for the Colonies when I get back. And you, my poor, unfortunate young man, what are you wearing?"

"Woollies," said Bones.

That was his last defiant gesture.

DON MURDOCH came to the territories with three guns and a breaking heart. At least he had tried to keep the rifts wedged open and still preserved the similitude of hopeless grief and unconquerable despair. It had been easy enough that night when the New York skyline was falling astern and he had looked over the side of the *Berengria* and had seen, almost on the verge of tears, the pilot's hazardous climb to the waiting boat.

This man, thought Donald, swallowing a lump in his throat, was going back to a woman who loved him. A sane, shrewd mother of children, who went to church on Sundays and scoffed at ghosts. He could not imagine Mr. Pilot and Mrs. Pilot facing one another, trembling with fury over the matter of manifestations.

He could not imagine Mrs. Pilot drawing her wedding ring from her finger, flinging it on to the table and saying: "I think we are wasting time, Donald: you cannot understand and never will understand. You are just puffed up with conceit like every other college boy—you think people are crazy because you haven't the vision or the enterprise to get outside your own narrow circle . . ."

All that sort of stuff, mostly illogical, but very, very poignant.

So Donald went tragically to the wilds and made a will before leaving New York, leaving half of his four million dollars to Jane Fellaby and the other half to found a society for the suppression of Spiritualism.

Jane had been bitten very badly. She had sat in at séances and had heard voices and seen trumpets move and heard tambourines play, and had had other spiritual experiences. And she objected to his description of Professor Steelfit as a "fake" and her spiritualistic aunt as a half-wit—and here he was sailing for Africa, the home of primitive realities and lions and fever.

Mr. Commissioner Sanders did not like visitors in the Territories. They were a responsibility, and usually he ran them up to Chubiri on the lower river (which is as safe as Bond Street and much safer than Broadway) and sent them back to the ship with a thrilling sense of having faced fearful dangers.

Bones was usually the guide on these occasions.

"On your right, dear old friends, is the village of Goguba, where there was a simply fearful massacre . . . shockin' old bird named N'sumu used to be chief an' the silly old josser got tight an' behaved simply scandalously. On the left, dear young miss, is the island where all these old johnnies are buried . . . over there's where a perfectly ghastly feller named Oofaba drowned his naughty old self . . ."

But the "tourist" with letters of introduction was not really welcome, though he or she had little to complain of in the matter of courtesy and loving-kindness.

"Bones, here's a job for you." Sanders looked up from the letters he was reading at breakfast. "We are getting a 'Cook' for a couple of weeks."

Bones sighed audibly.

"Not me, dear old excellency," he begged. "It's Ham's turn."

"He's an American," said Sanders.

Bones was interested.

He knew America. There was scarcely a town in the United States to which he had not written for Folder K, for Lieutenant Tibbetts was a most assiduous reader of magazine advertisements, and his touching faith in the efficacy of correspondence schools had produced his most expensive hobbies.

Sanders might not like visitors, but he had a particularly keen admiration for wholesome youth, and Donald Murdock was one of those shy and diffident boys whose appeal was instant.

He came with the most unusual credentials—a letter from the American Ambassador in London, supported by a request from Whitehall which was a command.

"Yes—you can go as far as you like, Mr. Murdock—which I hope will be as far as *I* like! The country is quiet and Mr. Tibbetts will look after you."

Youth cleaves to youth: Donald took up his quarters in Bones' hut. Within five hours of their meeting (the visitor arrived by the mail boat in the afternoon) they were swopping love affairs.

". . . not like any other girl, you understand, Bones. If she'd been one of those gosh-awful creatures that take up spiritualism, it wouldn't have mattered."

"I knew a girl once," mused Bones. "She was fearfully fond of me, but she played bridge. I said to her: 'My dear old lady——' "

But Donald Murdock really wasn't interested.

"When a man like me falls in love, Bones, it's for keeps. Spiritualism! Can you beat that? Ghosts and things—you don't believe in that kind of bunk?"

Here Bones hesitated.

"Dear old transatlantic cousin," he said, "you can't live in Africa and not believe, old boy."

Don Murdock stared at him incredulously.

"Spirits?"

Bones nodded.

"Dear old man from Massa—whatever the place is—ghosts? Lord bless my jolly old life, I've seen 'em!"

There were ghosts enough on the river, as these two young men were to learn.

There was a king of the N'gombi who had seven sons and the youngest of these was a weakling who had never been heard to utter a word until he was twelve, though there were tales told by huntsmen who had seen him in the forest, where he loved to prowl, of a ghost with whom he spoke at great length.

They had spied on him on nights of moon, and had heard him talk to one whom their eyes could not see, though they were trained to find the twigs which the big cat leopard had broken with his velvet paw.

Now the brothers of this boy would have put him away because of his madness, for this is the law of the N'gombi, that the mad are dead minds which are chained to the earth. But the king of the N'gombi (who was a very sick man) liked his son, who was the child of his best loved wife, and to those who sat in family palaver on this matter of life and death he spoke with a certain ominous meaning.

"The day B'lala dies, which of you shall live?" he asked. "For if I say 'kill' a hundred spears will go against any man even if he be the king's son."

B'lala began talking at large when he was thirteen. He talked of ghosts and ju-jus and strange things that only ghosts see. Such as elephants with long hairy skin and curved tusks, and crocodiles that flew from one great tree to another, and strange beasts with enormous necks and silly spade-shaped heads. Once he said that he had lived in the world when it was quivering, boiling mud and there was nothing to be seen, no sky or stars or sun, because of the thick steam that enveloped all things.

N'kema, the eldest son of the king, on the pretext of fishing, drew his brethren to a secret conference on one of the little islands.

"It is clear to me that our father will soon die and that the madness of B'lala is his madness also. Now all men know that I shall sit in his place and be king of the N'gombi. Yet when Sandi came at the third moon to gather our taxes, he spoke evilly to me because of some girl that I stole from the Ochori folk. Now I saw with these two eyes"—he covered them both with his palms in the conventional manner—"that whilst Sandi spoke to me, B'lala stood near to him and bewitched him with his magic. Now when our father dies, let us take B'lala into the forest and put out his eyes and leave him to the beasts."

And all the brothers agreed except one who loved the boy, and even he said "Wa," keeping his objection secret.

Mr. Commissioner Sanders, in his great white house by the river's end, heard these stories and was interested. He had an overwhelming weakness for sanity, but mad folk did not irk him unless they held high posts and could in their craziness call their spears to a killing.

"It is very queer," he puffed thoughtfully at a long cheroot—"I must take a peep at this boy on my next visit."

Captain Hamilton of the King's Houssas grinned.

"That corner of the N'gombi is rotten with madness," he said. "They had sleepy sickness badly last year——"

Sanders' head shake interrupted him.

"It isn't that kind of madness," he said. "B'lala's visions are of the world in the course of its creation and development. His talk is scientifically sound; he has even described the reptilia—

"The mammoth herds and the lizard birds,"

and that isn't right. In other words, he seems to have the extraordinary power of projecting his mentality back to prehistoric times. I can see you are on the point of saying 'rubbish'—don't! I had a go of fever last night and my temper is short."

Hamilton's nose wrinkled derisively.

"Sorry, sir. Ask Bones for a solution—he's nearly imbecile himself—he may be able to interpret his brother half-wit."

He raised himself in his chair and hailed a distant figure.

"Bones!" he yelled.

Lieutenant Tibbetts, of the King's Houssas, changed direction and came stalking across the drill ground. He took the three steps of the verandah in his stride and saluted formally.

"Do, you wish to see me on any regimental matter, dear old officer?" he demanded stiffly. "Personal affairs I am not prepared to discuss, but I hope, dear old sir, that I know enough about King's Regulations to be respectful, dear old tyrant——"

"Shut up," snapped Hamilton. "Anyway you did pinch my tooth-paste."

"I may have borrowed it, sir an' captain," said Bones gently, "thinkin' that you had no use for it——"

"You *did* take it," growled Hamilton. "I wouldn't have made a fuss about that, but you brought back a tube of brown shoe polish, and the first thing I knew —ugh!"

Bones inclined his head.

"Accidents will happen, dear old sir." He was offensively respectful. "I said to our jolly old North American friend——"

Sanders had an idea.

"Bones, take the *Wigle* up to the N'gombi country—we've got to give Murdock some sort of trip, and the country is quiet just now—I'd like you to see B'lala, the son of Ufumbi the king. . . ." He explained at length his interest in the boy.

"Anyway, he's crazy," said Donald gloomily. "Mr. Sanders says he's crazy— you can't see ghosts any other way."

"I've seen ghosts, dear old septic," said Bones stiffly.

"You mean sceptic," corrected the melancholy Donald. "What sort of education do they give you in your high schools?"

"A jolly sight better than they give you in your public schools," said Bones hotly, and was nearer the truth than he imagined.

They were sitting on the foredeck of the *Wigle* , that stout launch, and the low-lying shores of the Isisi country were moving slowly past them. It was the third day of the voyage, and hot—hotter than anything Donald had ever experienced, though as a loyalist he praised New York on a sweltering summer day as having it beaten. At Lapori, where he stopped, Bones had news that nearly sent him to the right-about.

"Lord, in the dark hours there came a lokali message from the N'gombi," said the old headman. "The king has died of the sickness *mong* , and his son is in his place. Also fishermen who came down the river have seen N'gombi war canoes and spears, and it is a saying on the river that when the N'gombi goes on the water, there are new graves on the little island."

Bones scratched his chin thoughtfully. In a moment of mental aberration he had forgotten to bring his carrier pigeons.

"This is a bad palaver," he said. "Get me a fast canoe, with strong young paddlers, and I will send a book[B] to my lord Sandi."

[B]

letter.

In the ordinary relationships of life Bones was as inconstant as an English spring day. But Bones, faced with real trouble and real responsibility was a being transfigured. He counted heads, and found himself with five effective fighting men besides himself and Donald. Fortunately the *Wiggle* carried one very desirable "spare" in the shape of a machine-gun, and this he had unpacked and erected on the foredeck. Mr. Donald Murdock was intensely interested.

"Dear old thing," said Bones, "you can paddle downstream in the canoe, or you can risk the fearfully hazardous dangers of war. I realize, dear old Massachuter, that you're a friendly nation, but if you like to come in you'll be fearfully welcome. If there's any last message you'd like to send to jolly old Jane, now's your chance."

Donald elected for war. An hour later the *Wiggle* pushed her sharp nose against the black waters of the river and began her laborious "climb" against the six-knot current to the river-city of the N'gombi.

Power is a potent wine that is liable to turn the heads of the strongest. N'kema, the eldest son did many foolish things. The breath was scarcely out of the body of his father—who died with suspicious suddenness—than he sat himself on the stool of chieftainship and summoned all headmen and petty chiefs to a great palaver of the land. Worse than this, he conveyed to the Little Leopards his desire for their support, and no king in his senses would invoke the aid of that secret society.

It was the time when the Little Leopards flourished; no longer were their mutilated victims found, but they had their strange rites, their dances, and, if the truth be told, their secret killings.

When one of the brothers expostulated the new king cut him short.

"Must I not bring all magic and power to keep me where I am?" he asked. "Does not Sandi hate me? Now, if he sees my strength, and knows that all men are for me, he will let me sit quietly, and one day will come and put on my neck the medal which my father wore."

"What of B'lala?" asked one, and the king made a significant sign.

That night two of his brothers led the ghost-walker into the deepest part of the forest, where slinking cat shapes move by night and round green moons of eyes look hungrily through the cover of the scrub; and there they left him. He did not complain, except to say, just before they went away:

"You would not have done this, but my Ghost is gone from me to-night."

"Where is your ghost?" mocked one.

"In all the stars," was the answer—"Go quickly before he returns."

And in terror they fled.

The new king sat in his big hut, an eager listener to all the stories which came to him. Some said that the Ochori were arming against the N'gombi, and that Bosambo the king was gathering his regiments for a great slaughter. Another whispered of Sandi and his soldiers. Yet another spoke of plots made by his own brothers to put him down. So it came about that the maimers of B'lala had scarcely returned to the city before they were seized and hurried away and no man saw them again.

The new king sat and listened, and with every fresh tale his fear grew.

His city was an armed camp. Spearmen answered the frantic summons of the *lokali* and came flocking through the forests and the swamps to join the army that was assembling.

"Lord, with whom do we war?" asked an old counsellor.

"All the world," said the shivering king.

Some sycophant whispered that the counsellor was an enemy or why should he ask this question, and that night the old man was killed in his hut.

Just before the dawn the king was awakened, and came out of his hut to find a sweating messenger. The king listened, his teeth chattering; and a frightened man is a terribly dangerous man. He sent for his familiars and gave them brief instructions.

"Tibbetti, the son of Sandi, is coming with his soldiers. Let all the men go to the forest with their spears, and he who is seen by Tibbetti I will surely kill!"

The *Wigle* came to a peaceable landing beach, where women were dipping their babies in the river and others were beating their clothes upon flat stones. There was no sign of warlike preparation when Bones stepped ashore; indeed, the atmosphere was favourable as N'kema the king came hurrying down to meet his visitor.

"Lord Tibbetti," he said, his eyes roving the deck for the soldiers, "you come at a good time, for my father is dead, and all the people with one voice have called me to sit in his seat. Now I will make a great dance for you and for your brother."

He was puzzled by the presence of Donald, a stranger, and found the most likely explanation for his presence.

"There will be no dances, N'kema," said Bones curtly. "And as to who shall sit on the king's chair, that is for Sandi. I come now to see B'lala, the king's son."

There was a dead silence. The chief's discomfort was all too apparent.

"Lord," he said, "this boy has gone a long journey, for he was sick, and on the edge of the Isisi."

"He shall be here to-morrow," said Bones. "The palaver is finished."

34

He walked through the village and was relieved to find none of the evidence of feverish activity which invariably marked a change of kingship. As for Mr. Murdock, he was frankly disappointed.

"Where's your old war?" he demanded truculently.

"Dear old sir," shuddered Bones, "don't talk about it."

That afternoon, as they sat on the deck under a double canvas shade, there came an emissary of the king to offer again the honour of a great dance, and this time Bones accepted.

"Shall we see any ghosts?" asked Donald hopefully.

"You don't see our kind of ghosts, old boy," replied Bones testily, "you feel 'em!"

Again he spoke prophetically.

The dance passed without incident, and the two loaded automatics in Bones' pocket seemed to be a superfluous precaution. They made their way back in the dark to the ship's side, and for the moment Donald Murdock was so entranced by the queer gyrations he had witnessed that he forgot that there was such a fake in the world as spiritualism.

They had said good-night when from the darkness of the bank came a sibilant whisper. Bones craned his head forward and listened.

"Tell him to come into my little ship," he ordered, and they brought into his tiny cabin the second younger son of the old king, he who had demurred at the destruction of his brother; and the story he had to tell struck all the boredom from Lieutenant Tibbetts' face.

"Lord, if the king knows I have been, he will kill me as he has slain my brother," said the man fearfully. "But I tell you this because I love Sandi, and because, when he comes to make a chief, he will not forget a son of the king who has helped him."

"Where did they take B'lala?" asked Bones, and the man told him.

"But, lord, if you go through the woods behind the city, they will kill you," urged the man, "for there are more warriors than trees, and each man is strong for my brother."

Bones did not hesitate. He had a short consultation with Murdock.

"You'll stay here, my dear old New Yorker," he said. "This naughty old feller won't do anything to-night——"

"I'm coming along with you," said Donald recklessly, and in the end his insistence prevailed.

They dropped into a small canoe, paddled softly down the river for a mile and, landing at a convenient place (here Donald nearly fell into the water) followed their guide for two hours through the dense woods which had hidden murders from time immemorial. Once green eyes glared at them ahead; once Donald heard the scream of a monkey in the grip of an invisible enemy.

It was midnight by the illuminated dial on Murdock's wrist when they came to a little clearing and saw a figure in the moonlight, reclining against a big, lightning-blasted tree.

35

"O B'lala," said Bones softly, "I am Tibbetti, the son of Sandi, and I have come to take you away to my fine ship."

He saw the thick lips of the child twist in a smile—guessed rather than saw the horror of his eyes.

"Lord, I go to a better place than your fine ship," he said faintly, "for this night I shall walk among the stars with my new ghost. Do I speak truth?"

At first Bones thought he was addressing him, but saw the head turn slightly to the left and heard the delighted chuckle of the dying boy.

"Lord," he said, "I speak truth. Now I tell you, Tibbetti, that there is death in this wood, for this my great ghost has told me; also I saw you coming—I who have no eyes! You came in a little boat with my brother, and as you landed, the white man who is with you stumbled and fell."

Donald felt a cold shiver run down his spine.

"Who told you this?" he said, in English, and, to Bones' amazement, this boy, who had never spoken any language but his own, answered:

"He who is by you!"

Again he turned his head.

"Lord Ghost, stay with Tibbetti and his friend, and be strong for them."

He waited, his head bent, as though he were listening. Bones saw him nod and again heard the delighted chuckle. Then he turned his head.

"Lord Tibbetti," he said, "my ghost has spoken, and he will be with you till you come to your journey's end, and he will be strong for you."

They waited for a long time, and when he did not speak Bones stooped and laid the figure gently on the ground.

"Humph!" he said, and got up, for he knew that B'lala, the friend of ghosts, was walking amongst the stars.

They buried him as best they could and trekked back to the river. Bones knew that there was only one hope, and that was to cast off the boat at once, risk shoals and sandbanks, and steam through the night to meet Sanders. A night in the native mind was an eternity. Perhaps N'kema would strike before dawn.

He struck earlier, as it proved. They were within half a mile of the village when a hoarse voice challenged them.

"Stand for the Little Leopard, white man!"

"Shoot!" snarled Bones, and whipped out his automatic.

The forest rang with the staccato crash of shots. Bones went down under three N'gombi warriors and waited expectantly for the end. Something struck him on the head. . . .

It was the consciousness of pain which revived him. The sun was up, and he was sitting with his back to a slim tree, his arms most painfully drawn back, and knotted on the tree's other side; and within a few feet of him sat Mr. Donald Murdock, naked to the waist and bearing marks of battle.

"Hullo, you alive? . . . I thought they'd bumped you off," he said cheerfully. "What are they going to do?"

Bones turned his aching head left and right. They were entirely surrounded by spearmen; and sitting on his stool of chieftainship immediately before them, was N'kema the king.

"O Tibbetti, I see you!" he mocked. "Where is the great ghost of my little mad brother? Is he not by you and will not his strong arm be against me and my young men?"

Bones was puzzled: how did the king know of the meeting in the forest and all that the dying boy had said?

And then his eyes fell on something brown and still that lay in the long grass . . . a wisp of smoke curled up near by . . . the brother of the king, who had led him to B'lala, had told before he too found in death a pleasant relief.

"I see you, N'kema," he said hoarsely, for his throat was parched; "and as to madmen and ghosts, are you not mad to do this evil thing, and will not your ghost go weeping on the mountains when Sandi comes? Yet I will speak well for you and leave a book for Sandi, if you let this young man go." He nodded towards the uncomprehending Murdock, for Bones was speaking in the dialect of the N'gombi. "For he belongs to a strange people and has no part in this palaver."

N'kema grinned fearfully.

"O ko! That is the talk of a fool. Now let me see your ghost, Tibbetti. And if he is strong he shall hold the arm of my slayer."

He spat left and right and lifted his hand to his eyes. It was the signal to the lithe warrior who squatted at his feet, bending the supple execution knife in his hands. Up to his feet he rose and came swiftly before Bones.

"Speak well for me to all ghosts and devils," he muttered conventionally, and swung back his arm.

Bones glared up at him and did not flinch. The curved knife glittered in the sunlight, and then. . . .

Bones heard a little thud, saw the knife drop from the man's hand, as he gripped a bloody elbow with a shriek of pain.

N'kema was on his feet, grey-brown.

"O ko!" he gasped. "This ghost. . . !"

And then he saw Sanders.

The Commissioner was standing on the edge of the clearing, and on each side of him knelt six tarboshed Houssas, their rifles levelled. Slowly Sanders walked across the open and the armed throng flowed back noiselessly, each man seeking the kindly obscurity of the forest.

"I see you, N'kema."

Sanders' voice was low, almost caressing. And then he pointed to a tree, and Sergeant Abiboo, who walked behind him, flung the rope he carried, so deftly that the noose slipped down over the smooth branch almost to the level of N'kema's neck.

• • • • •

"Ghosts—phew!" Donald wiped his brow. "Did you see . . . just as this bird was going to strike . . . something stopped him . . . that beats everything."

Bones coughed. He had seen the new silencers on the Houssas' rifles.

"We've got a pretty bright brand of bogies, dear old thing," he said.

Murdock shook his head.

"I've got a new slant on this spiritualistic business. There was something there—I'll swear it. . . . Gosh! it was more awful than being carved up!"

"A common phenomenon, dear old Atlantist," murmured Bones.

"I'm going to cable Jane and say I'm strong for spiritualism if you get the right brand."

As it happened, it was unnecessary. The Eurasian operator handed him a cablegram as he arrived at headquarters:

> "You are right. Spooks are bunk. Experts found professor's finger marks on tin trumpet. Come home."
>
> "JANE."

Donald shook his head.

"I've got to convince that girl," he said.

BREAKFAST time was the hour of controversy at the residency. It was most vehement when Captain Hamilton of the King's Houssas had a little touch of liver, or was recovering from the effects of a bout of fever.

Lieutenant Tibbetts could also be very annoying. He was constantly rediscovering obvious things, or revivifying theories that had been decently interred in the year dot. Never a trip did he make to the hinterland but he brought back some marvellous recovery of that which had never been lost.

"As to the sceptre of the great king—stuff, Bones! That old yarn has been dead a hundred years," snapped Hamilton. "There never was such a thing, and you know jolly well that native chiefs, whether they call themselves kings or princes or just ordinary trumpery lieutenants——"

"Thank you," murmured Bones, closing his eyes and displaying every evidence of Christian resignation.

"Anyway, they had never had—sceptres—or orbs."

"Or thrones?" asked Bones significantly. "Dear, old officer, be reasonable! Thrones, old boy, are in the Bible—you can't get away from it. And sceptres, too. I'm absolutely sure, old boy, that one of these old johnnies has got his tucked away. Bosambo says——"

"Bosambo is a liar, and the maniacal credulity of his dupes is beyond understanding."

"Thank you again, sir and captain," said Bones.

And here Sanders stepped in.

"I've heard the yarn hundreds of times, Bones. Haven't they threatened me with the Great King's sceptre ever since I've been here? Aren't the nations all to be united under one great monarch who will drive us into the sea? And have six months passed without an amateur rising and saying 'Behold, I am the man?' There have been more wars over that infernal sceptre—they call it 'stick,' by the way—than any other general cause I can remember."

"Thank you for your collaboration, dear old Excellency."

" 'Corroboration' is the word you want," interrupted Hamilton.

"Thank you, Excellency and friend," said Bones, taking no notice of his chief. "And now I'll tell you something—Bosambo has seen it!"

He said this with an air of drama, flourished an arm and stepped back to watch the effect. Nobody did very much.

"Bosambo's never seen anything but—oh, what's the use?"

Bones smiled pityingly. He had faith in the Great King's sceptre, and had dreams of discovering it one day, and of taking his children to the British Museum, and there, under a glass case upon red velvet, or possibly blue, this mystic symbol of power would be displayed, and on a gilt-edged card placed on the other side, so that you might see it whichever way you went round the case (and possibly at each end), the inscription: "Presented to the Nation by Lieutenant Tibbetts, Fellow of the Royal Geographical Society." There would follow a short biography which began:

"This daring explorer, whose name is a household word. . . ."

And as he dreamt, all things conspired to bring the King's sceptre into being.

The people of the Akasava had no liking for foreigners, and woe to the Isisi fishermen who poached upon their waters! Yet they took readily enough to M'turi, son of O'faka, son of Mofobama-N'kema, because his father was the greatest of all the Isisi seers, and had prophesied mighty wars and famines and strange signs in the sky; and then he prophesied the death of the King of the Isisi so vividly and convincingly that Sanders in his far-away residence came quickly in his little ship, only just in time to save the king from the effects of aconite poisoning. After he had hanged the seer, and had delivered an interesting lecture to all chiefs and headmen on the unprofitable character of prophecy, a reaction set in, and M'turi, who was no seer but a vain and handsome man, fled to the Akasava and by them was received courteously, for, as they say on the river, the Isisi love women, the Ochori love food, but the Akasava starve for goats.

Now M'turi the hunter had no occult powers, but he was a shrewd man; and one day, when hunting monkeys on the far south in what was indubitably Isisi country, he came to one side of a narrow ravine through which the river ran rapidly. Here the stream was narrow. It was indeed one of the many Hell's Gates that the river knew.

There were seven places so called on the Great River. It sounded grand and thrillingly profane, and each man who named a little canyon had infinite faith in his originality. In the main the river is terribly broad, and its bed is humped in strange and tantalizing places with great sandbanks which have a knack of disappearing in the time of flood and turning up to the discomfort of navigators in those parts of the river where hitherto there had been deep water and a clear channel. But in three of the gates the river ran narrow and strong between high banks. Such ravines are by no means safe in storm time, and it was a standing order to all chiefs and headmen that they should report any sign of insecure banking.

M'turi was tired. He lit a little fire and cooked the leg of a monkey, deciding to sleep on the ground and return to the Akasava city the next morning. He was uneasy, too, for he had heard that the king was weary of harbouring a magician who worked no magic.

Before he rolled himself in the monkey skin robe that early evening, he walked to the precipice and sat with his legs dangling over the edge, with a sheer drop of a hundred feet below. As he sat, he felt himself slightly swaying, as though the ground were moving backward and forward in gentle motion. And that could not be for he was sitting on a great rock embedded in the earth. All his senses acute, he concentrated his mind upon the motion. And then he saw what caused the swaying. There was a high wind, and the ground moved in unison with two tall Isisi palms which were swaying to and fro. They were distant from him nearly fifty yards, and, rising, he walked back.

The palms grew in a deep cleft of earth, and he realized that the whole of the ledge was one great rock, so delicately poised that the movement of the palm trunks against it was sufficient to set it gently rocking. He followed the cleft, recognized it as a breakaway, and knew that it would be only a matter of weeks or months before that mass of stone crashed down into the river.

M'turi went back the next morning to the Akasava city, where he had nearly overstayed his welcome; for he had prophesied nothing, seen no ghosts, pointed out no man or woman in whom little devils had their habitation.

And he arrived in time for a palaver of elders.

There had been a slight collision between some huntsmen of the Ochori and some huntsmen of the Akasava in the northern Akasava territory. Nobody was completely killed, but Bosambo, the chief of the Ochori, went swiftly to the edge of his territory and summoned the paramount chiefs of the Akasava to meet him near the four gum trees which from time immemorial has been the palaver place of the two nations. Such was the influence of Bosambo that the chiefs came, albeit with some reluctance.

Right was on the side of Bosambo. The Akasava had been hunting in forbidden territory, and Mr. Commissioner Sanders was swift to punish such trespass by fines and national impositions.

"Lord Bosambo, this is the truth," said the chief of the Akasava. "My young men have been led into their bad ways by a foreigner, M'turi of the Isisi, who lives in my city. This night I will send him back to his people and beat him for his wickedness."

Bosambo said nothing, knowing full well that, but for the magic of Sanders' name, there would be trouble with which he could not cope, for half his territory was in a mild condition of rebellion over the matter of a hut tax which Bosambo had imposed, and he smelt that the chief of the Akasava was ripe for war.

The chief of the Akasava came back to his city in no good mood.

"I tell you, M'turi, that you have brought shame upon the Akasava. For that dog Bosambo, whose father was a slave . . ." (he also particularized the mother), "has mocked me as though I were a child or an old man. And but for Sandi I would have taken my spears to his country and there would have been sad hearts in the Ochori. Now we gave you our hut and our food because you were the son of your father, but you have given us no magic nor told us of the great things which are coming to us."

"Lord chief," said M'turi, "hear me! Take your spears to the Ochori, and Sandi shall not come, nor his little ship, nor his guns which say 'ha-ha.' For great magic shall happen, and my ju-ju shall stand in the river and no little ship shall pass him."

"That is the talk of a fool," said the chief of the Akasava angrily.

That night they gave him a worn-out canoe, a day's supply of food, and an ancient paddle, and M'turi's heart was hot with anger against the Akasava for the rudeness of their send-off.

When he had drawn from the shore and gone out of sight of the watchers, he made a wide circle, crept back to the beach where the best of the Akasava canoes were laid, and, taking the finest, he paddled his way up stream, hiding and sleeping by day, and presently came to the Ochori country.

He was brought into the presence of Bosambo, and squatted at the big man's feet.

"I see you, Bosambo!" he said. "Now I am M'turi, the son of the great O'faka of the Isisi, and because of my father's magic I have come to make a great prophecy. You shall take your spears into the Akasava country and you shall be king of all this land, of the Akasava and of the Isisi. For I have a powerful ju-ju which will stand in the way of Sandi and his soldiers, and his little white ship, and his guns that say 'ha-ha,' and this ju-ju will push them back, and you shall be lord of this land for ever."

Bosambo regarded the fine figure of M'turi with contempt. He spat left and right and spoke one word.

"Nigger," he said in English, and signalled the soldiers who stood about.

They took M'turi to the beach, confiscated such of his property as remained in the canoe, beat him with rhinoceros hide and sent him, sore and vengeful, down the river.

So, in some trepidation he came back to his own people, and built a hut aloof from the Isisi city, and was glad that the sins of his father had been forgotten and that the little boys did not mock him because of his father who was hanged. . . .

"There has been some sort of trouble between Bosambo and those infernal Akasava," said Sanders. "It seems to have been smoothed over, but if you happen to be in the neighbourhood, Bones, I wish you'd have a look round. You can take the *Zaire*, by the way; there's an engineer coming down to overhaul the *Wigle* ."

"If there's any trouble, dear old Excellency," said Bones gravely, "you can be perfectly certain that old Bones will use tact. At the same time, dear and revered Excellency, I'd be simply fearfully glad if you'd ask Captain Hamilton, who is my superior officer and a good fellow, and all that sort of thing, to keep his naughty old fingers from pickin' an' choosin'. I make no accusations against anybody, dear old Excellency," Bones went on, studiously avoiding the stern glance of his superior officer, "but I had four jars of preserved ginger sent to me by a well-beloved aunt—a simply topping old thing who lives at Weybridge—why she lives there I've never discovered, except that it's quite close to Brooklands ——"

"The only scrap of preserved ginger I've eaten was that which you offered to me on its arrival," said Hamilton. "I thought it was very inferior preserved ginger: in fact, it nearly made me sick."

Bones closed his eyes and smiled. He could be very tantalizing.

The next dawn the *Zaire* steamed out into the river, and Bones was content to leave the navigation of the river to Yoka, the engineer, for he was preparing a document for the press of Surrey—he even contributed the headlines:

STRANG AFFICAN AFRICAN FETTISH.

42

SEPTAR SCEPTER SCEAPTER OF
PREHISTORIC KING FOUND.

LT. TIBBETTS VALLUABLE AND
DUMFOUNDING DISCOVERRY.

Bones came to the edge of the Isisi country in turbulent weather. For three weeks there had been rain and high winds, thunderstorms by day and night. The river was swollen; the little Lolanga, its tributary, was now a foaming sea, and long before they reached the confluence Bones saw the yellow and the black streaking side by side, and was troubled. There were times when he could make no greater progress than two knots, other times when he could skirt the wide pools out of the current and resume normal progress.

He had reached Hell's Gate and, with the aid of a powerful lamp fixed to the bows, made his attempt to get through. The little *Zaire* trembled and shook from bow to stern, her two funnels belched a fiery trail of sparks, for here the current was at its strongest.

Soaked from head to foot in the rain which fell like a solid sheet, Bones stood by the steersman, his grave eyes fixed ahead. The *Zaire* won forward foot by foot; the waters piled up against her bow until the crest was within a few inches of the bulwarks.

Bones looked up anxiously at the banks from time to time: this was the season when queer things happened.

Hour followed hour, and the V-shaped mouth of the gorge was within cable length when he heard a roar and a crack, and, looking up, he saw what he thought was one whole bank collapsing. It fell over with incredible slowness, and then, with a report like the explosion of a gun, it fell. . . .

It missed the ship by a few feet—a shower of stones rattled down on the deck, and a fair-sized sapling, uprooted in the landslide, fell athwart the deck. This probably saved the *Zaire* from destruction, for a second later she was lifted on the crest of a huge wave and flung against the rocky face of the canyon. The bushy end of the tree acted as fender—the force jerked the trunk up like a stick—in another moment the steamer was flung forward clear of the canyon.

"Gracious heavens alive!" gasped Bones.

He came haggardly to the beach of the Isisi city at dawn, and B'fundi, the old man, brought for the admiration of Tibbetti his new bride whom men called The Wonderful Walker.

On the edge of the Alamandi country, where live the strange tribes who pay no taxes and owe no allegiance to any man or system, dwelt an N'gombi fisherman who had seven daughters, all of whom were straight-backed and pretty walkers. The trained mannequins of the Paris ateliers are awkward and cow-like in their movements compared with an N'gombi maid, and the daughters of Boliki, the fisherman, were famous even amongst their own kind for the supple rhythm of their bodies.

So that women came from their villages to visit the five huts on the banks of the shallow Sagar River to learn from the children of Boliki how a woman might walk and yet glide as though she stood firmly and it was the ground that moved beneath her.

B'fundi of the Isisi, who was a rich old man, so near to dissolution that his foolishness was applauded by those who hoped to share his wealth, heard of the pretty walkers and came in his fine canoe to the village of Boliki, saw the seven daughters and married them, leaving Boliki well satisfied with the treasures that had been paid for the girls, and more satisfied because these riches gave him title to a new wife.

So came B'fundi to his own village.

All his sons who had worked for him and had given their best, who had hunted in the forest and brought him the skins, who had journeyed miles through strange lands and brought him back rubber, who had chaffered for goats, and at his order had sweated against the current to buy richly nurtured dogs for his table, saw the walker, and neither approved nor disapproved of her, regarding her as a toy in the hands of death.

The people of the Isisi came in from outlying towns and cities and villages to watch this girl glide down the broad centre street, the men squatting with their clenched fists to their teeth, frowning, the women agog that anybody could walk so beautifully.

Time passed, and the wonder of the walker had melted long before Bones brought the *Zaire* to beach, and the women who had tried to imitate her had ceased from their efforts, so that when Lilaga walked along the street men did not so much as turn their heads, and only the chattering and malicious women made unprintable references to her gait.

But in the house of the old man B'fundi there was great soreness of heart, for Lilaga the beautiful walker had charmed this old man by that devil which was supposed to lie behind the centre of her starry eyes. And every day she asked for something, and every day he gave it.

Now those who had watched her arrival had seen M'turi, the hunter, standing on the foreshore a little aloof, leaning on his spear, a tall, wonderful man, whose muscles rippled under his brown satin skin with every movement; and they had seen Lilaga look at him, and he looked at her. And some said that in the dead of the night this wonderful walker glided unseen to the lonely hut of M'turi, which stood far aloof from the village; but whether the scandal was justified or not, this was known, that M'turi, who was a poor man, became suddenly a rich man. His pens became filled with edible dogs, and his goats were many; he had great sacks of salt and brass bangles, and a bed of skin, and other wonders which only come to the old and the thrifty.

One moonless night, Lilaga the walker met M'turi on the edge of the forest and walked before him to his hut. In her hand she had a small bag that jingled pleasantly.

"This is the treasure which he had buried under his bed, and which he gave for the love of me," she said.

But M'turi had other matters to talk about.

"This night I heard the lokali and it said that in the narrow-narrow river there is no river any more, only earth and rocks, and to-morrow will come Tibbetti. Now, you are very clever, Lilaga, and your husband is well liked by Tibbetti, who will come soon with his soldiers. You shall find for me if Sandi has magic to clear the river. And if he has, you shall steal it for me. And I will be a great man amongst the Isisi and we will live in your husband's hut, for he will be dead, and we will divide his riches."

Sanders came five days afterwards in response to the urgent pigeon post that Bones had sent. And with him the providential engineer who had come to overhaul the *Wiggle* . The Commissioner had received the message in time to collect stores from the ship that carried the engineer to the territories, and the patched-up *Wiggle* brought back tackle, stores and men, and a camp was made near the principal city of the Isisi, where B'fundi had built three great huts for his lord.

He was a wise man, and very old, and his wealth was incredible. So powerful was he by this reason that not even the predatory kings of the Isisi interfered with him or sought more than their legal tribute. Moreover, because of his great age, he was credited with magical powers. Some said that he could, by a snap of his fingers, produce the most terrifying variety of ghosts.

On the night of nights, that terrific culmination of the month of storms, when every hut in the city was damaged, and half of them laid low by a devastating wind, when the cornfields of overnight were masses of crushed stalks in the morning, and drowned dogs floated belly-up, B'fundi's houses were unharmed, and his dog pens were full of yelping beasts, and his corn stood high and proudly, as though they knew their master was a familiar of M'shimba-M'shamba, the great lord.

"Magic I have, and I often speak with ghosts," he told Sanders complacently; "but they are of a gentle kind and do no more than stroke my nose and tell me I shall live longer than the world. But you certainly must be a great magician if you can lift that big stone where M'shimba has laid it."

This he said, being instigated thereto by his wife.

"This I will do," said Sanders easily. "Some day my great ghost will come, and he will bark like a gun, and all the stone will fly upwards and outwards, so that if any man stand on the shore he will be killed. And then the river will go its own way."

B'fundi heard, but did not believe.

"Lord," he said, "in the Akasava they say that soon there will be no law; for this stone has fallen by their magic, so that your little ship, and your soldiers, and your guns that say 'ha-ha' cannot go to them. And they will do what they think best and send no tribute to you, neither rubber, nor fish, nor goats, nor salt."

Sanders smiled unpleasantly.

"So many men have talked as foolishly, B'fundi, and where are they? Their huts have grown into the grass, and their white bones have been washed out of the ground by the rains. I, also, am a wonderful walker," he added significantly, for he had heard of the daughter of Boliki, and perhaps of M'turi.

He yielded to the solicitations of B'fundi and showed him certain marvels. He felt that Bones could have played showman better, but Bones he had sent to the Ochori city with the *Zaire* and all the men he could spare.

"O ko!" said B'fundi, when Sanders had explained.

Later he told his wife, and she carried the news to M'turi, who stole one night to the store hut when the Houssa recruit who was on sentry was flirting with a woman, and he took away with him the magic rod that frees the beds of rivers.

Half-way back to his hut Lilaga, the wife of B'fundi, intercepted him.

"This night Tibbetti has sent word to Sandi, and soldiers are looking for you. Go quickly to the Akasava."

Again the hunted M'turi took to the river. He came with his great plot and his magic rod to the King of Akasava, who was quaking with fear because Tibbetti sat on the edge of his lands, and had soldiers and guns. So to propitiate his master the Akasava chief seized upon M'turi and sent him to Bosambo.

The prisoner arrived at midnight. Bosambo listened and saw, and his heart leapt at the sight of the Magic Rod. For on the previous night he had been estranged from Tibbetti.

"Now praise be to God!" he said in Arabic, and, going to the *Zaire*, woke Bones.

"Lord Tibbetti——" he began.

"Go away," snarled Bones. "Oh man of lies, go away or I will whip you!"

"Lord, I have that which I had not got," pleaded Bosambo, round the edge of the cabin door. "And when last night I said I had forgotten where I had hidden the Sceptre of the Great King, I spoke true, though you said I was an evil man. But in the night, Tibbetti, I had a dream. . . ."

Bones came out in his pyjamas and listened with great interest.

• • • • •

It had not been so terribly difficult to free Hell's Gate of its stony boom as Sanders had feared. Here the river is very deep—so deep that in places its bottom has never been fathomed. A hundred tons of stone that rested on the bank was persuaded by hydraulic jacks and other means to slide sideways. . . .

Sanders sent his little steamer over the place where the rock had sunk, and his sounding lead could find no trace of it.

He went back to the residency, leaving word to Bones that he was to follow and bring with him one M'turi. And this Bones did. He came to headquarters three days after. Sanders was at dinner when Bones stalked in and flung something on the table.

"Sceptre, dear old officer! Search, pertinacity, dogged determination, Excellency. Original sceptre of Good King Wenceslas, or whatever his name was. One of the most fearfully important relics in the world. . . ."

He spoke with great earnestness, tapping the squat thing on the table to mark every sentence.

"Natives don't know what it means——"

"Bones!" Sanders' voice was very urgent. "Do you mind not tapping that stick of dynamite on the table?"

Bones went white, and dropped the stick as though it had burnt him.

"Dynamite, sir?" he said faintly. "Goo' lor'! I've been sleeping with it under my pillow."

Hamilton picked up the explosive and carried it to the river. And in the river he dropped it.

VI

IN THE MANNER OF LIPSTICK

IT WAS one of those glorious days at headquarters which occur in the spring of the year. A fresh, cool breeze blew in from the sea, swaying the fronds of the palms and raising lazy swirls of dust at hut corners.

Mr. Tibbetts stood before a small body of non-commissioned officers, a book in his hand, his monocle screwed into his left eye. From the fact that he wore his Sam Browne, and that a leather-scabbarded sword hung at his left hip, it could be inferred that he was engaged in official duties.

Sanders, standing by the rail of the residency stoep, asked a question.

"A lecture," said Hamilton grimly. "They don't know what he's driving at, and I'll bet he doesn't, either. So they're all square."

Bones was lecturing on the subject of field engineering.

"About which there is no man who knows less," said Hamilton, with a certain gloomy satisfaction.

He watched the party dismiss and saw Bones go off to his hut to put away his sword and belt. One of the lectured had to pass the residency, and him Hamilton beckoned.

"O tell me, corporal-man," he said, "what wonder did the lord Tibbetti tell you?"

The corporal grinned uneasily, and shuffled his bare feet in his embarrassment.

"Lord," he said at last, "he spoke of a great canal that was dug up in this land, so big that ships could pass from one world to another. But this we knew was a jest, so we did not take notice of it."

Hamilton nodded.

"Also . . . ?" he asked.

The corporal's black and shiny face beamed.

"Lord, he spoke of certain holes in the ground into which we Houssas could go so that our enemies could not shoot us. But when Sergeant Mahmet Ibn Hassan asked how could we dig holes in the Eburi Country, where every spade raises water, my lord Tibbetti said rude words to the sergeant. So that we knew he was jesting also."

When the man had gone, Hamilton lit a cheroot.

"Suez Canal! How the devil does he bring that into the ambit of military engineering?"

Bones hove in sight at that moment. He had a book and several papers under his arm. His face was rather grave.

"Lecture dismissed, sir."

He saluted, dropped his papers and book, and spent a little time chasing one of the former; the sea breeze had freshened.

"What has the Suez Canal got to do with it?"

Bones shrugged his shoulders.

"Dear old officer, that, I admit, comes into the category of tictacs and strategy. To-morrow we trot out jolly old strains and stresses."

Hamilton glanced at the book. It was not, as he had expected, a post-correspondence volume, but one issued by the War Office.

"Yes, dear old commander, I'm perfectly serious. It started when I was readin' about dear old Lipstic—I was sort of fired——"

"Dear old who?" demanded Sanders.

"Lipstic, Excellency an' sir. The jolly old boy who built the Suez Canal——"

"Lesseps," snarled Hamilton. "Gosh! Why can't you get a name right?"

"Names are nothing, dear old Ham," chided Bones gently. "Good old Lipstic's name lives in his jolly old canal. *Circumspice docet*, dear old boy: 'Look around this canal and that's my memorial,' dear old Ham."

Later that day came a deputation from the Akasava folk, who live to the westward of the Eburi, and they came with a grievance. Their spokesman, a tousled old man, spoke boldly and despairingly by turns. His name was K'saga, he was a notorious thief and ruled a village of outcasts. There were a score of these communities up and down the river, peopled by men and women who had fled from the justice of their outraged fellows.

K'saga had to tell a tale of stolen goats and stolen women—but the goats were rather important. And the culprits were, of course, the Eburi.

When he had finished, Sanders spoke.

"O K'saga, I do not know which is worse, the Eburi people, or you and your village. Now I tell you again to gather your people and I will take them to a cleaner land where none can rob them, and I will pass my hand over them and wipe clean their evil deeds, so that no man who has lost a wife, and none who desires to avenge a brother, shall do harm to you."

But K'saga rejected the suggestion. He himself had the blood of two cousins on his hands and preferred the miserable village over which he lorded to the finest city where he would sleep badly and start at every sound.

"Lord, these Eburi people are devils now, saying evil things about your lordship. What will it be when their old chief dies, and a woman rules them?"

"That is with me," said Sanders briefly, and dismissed the palaver with promises of investigation.

Though he was not aware of the fact, the old chief of the Eburi was already with his fathers, and a woman sat on the stool of kingship. Sanders learnt this fact on his way up river.

There was no part of his territories that he approached with greater circumspection than the Eburi. Up and down the river they were called by various names. To the rest of the Akasava folk they were "The Unreachables," to the N'gombi, "the proud-faced," which may be translated as insolent. They paid taxation as and when they wished, they came and stayed away from tribal palavers at their own sweet will. They raided and stole, moving across their marshes with an ease which led to the legend (still persisting in certain works of ethnology) that they were web-footed.

How much of K'saga's story was true he must discover for himself. Rumours had come to him that the outcasts were "chopping" women—cannibalism was the most difficult of all crimes to suppress. And complaints that women had been stolen might well mean that K'saga and his hideous cabal were preparing alibis in advance.

Here he was not far wrong, for the new queen of the Eburi was too interested in her position to bother about her miserable neighbour.

When the woman I'safi-M'lo'bini knew that she was to be chief of the Eburi, she celebrated the unique occasion by adopting the Christian religion, and was received into the Roman Church by a sceptical priest, who gave her the name of Theresa. He was sceptical because he knew his Theresa rather well, and that his doubts were justified was proved when, following her conversion, she held a great dance in honour of the moon, and caused her late father's seven wives to be whipped.

Father Martin, a bearded man who wore the habit of a Franciscan and a solar topee, came aboard the *Zaire* to take tea with the Commissioner. Over a pipe he expressed his opinions—which were mainly uncomplimentary to Theresa.

"I could have wished that the Baptists had her," he said, gloomily; "she's missionary trained, speaks English—which is a diabolical accomplishment in a native—she can even play the harmonium. But she's mischief from the top of her woolly head to the soles of her big feet. When I found her using a picture of Our Lady to cure one of her dancing boys of belly-ache, I nearly took a stick to her!"

Sanders was mildly amused. How Theresa came to be the one woman chief in his territory is simply explained. The Eburi folk were rabidly strong for tradition. Failing the succession of the eldest son, for the chieftainship was in every sense dynastic, the seventh daughter of the seventh son was invariably elected. For a hundred and five years the eldest sons had followed one another in succession. Theresa was the first woman chief that the Eburi had had since the year 1817.

"She'll settle down," he said, but as an act of precaution sent for the new chief.

Between the Eburi and the river is a march of twenty-seven miles, mostly through swamp, and it was not a journey lightly to be undertaken. He waited a week and then the answer came from the mouth of her councillor.

"Lord, the woman our chief is sick and cannot come," he said.

Sanders read defiance in the message, but he was patient. Theresa must reveal herself before he took stronger action. And he was particularly anxious to avoid trouble.

From the river the ground rises gradually until in the Eburi the woods stand nearly five hundred feet above the river level. In the circumstances it was surprising that the twenty-mile belt of marsh existed, but a rough survey revealed the cause. There was a sloping stratum of clay beneath the soggy ground; evidence of this was supplied by the high clay cliffs that overshadow the river near

Chumbiri; and it was under these cliffs that Sanders had anchored the *Zaire* whilst he waited for the answer to his summons.

The marsh had a military value: it was wholly impossible to approach the Eburi on its most accessible side, and it had no other. For to left and right of the "corridor" which led into the interior were the frontiers of the French possessions. In shape the Eburi land may be likened to a squat, wide-necked flask—the very word Eburi means "gourd." Near where the corridor approached the river was a saucer-shaped depression of land in which dwelt K'saga and his people, and him Sanders visited.

Once before he had had occasion to take an armed force into the country, and he never forgot the nightmare month he spent mostly ankle-deep in water. Here dwelt water snakes and huge leeches, and a family of crocodiles, the founders of which at some remote period must have travelled overland to this swampy paradise. There were certain paths, more or less intermittent, that connected the area with the outer world, but only at certain seasons of the year were they practicable. The officer commanding troops, who made a visit of inspection, expressed the opinion that the country was almost impregnable.

It was a dirty village, clumsily and lazily built. No two huts were in line; the gardens where corn grew straggled into the unreclaimed waste. Men vanished at the sight of the dapper, white-clad figure, and even K'saga seemed to have an accusing conscience, for he was trembling when Sanders approached him.

The Commissioner made a tour of the village, looking for certain signs of guilt—incidentally choosing a tree on which he would hang K'saga if he found evidence of cannibalism. There was no proof, however. He went back to his ship and arrived in time to receive Theresa's second message.

It was decidedly insolent, and embodied a demand for "a great present." It was the first direct act of defiance which the Eburi people had delivered for close on twenty years. Sanders was not angry.

"Go back to the woman," he said, "and say that Sandi sends her this beautiful present, that she may see every day the face of one who will answer for all that happens in this land."

He handed the messenger a gaudily framed mirror, and went down the river, a very thoughtful man.

He had hardly arrived at headquarters when he summoned what was practically a council of war.

"This woman is going to give trouble. I've had information that she intends to re-establish the old sacrifices. That I will not stomach even if it costs me an expeditionary force. The only chance is that I can overawe her, and I purpose sending Bones in the *Wigle* with twenty men and a couple of machine-guns to establish a post on the edge of the marsh. There is a good camping ground near the clay bluff—also you can keep your eye on K'saga, who, I am certain, is chopping women. I've half a mind to send to headquarters for an engineer to make a survey of that section——"

"Dear old Excellency," murmured Bones, hurt, "headquarters . . . jolly old engineer . . . really, really!"

He rolled his head, a picture of injured pride.

"Leave it to Bones," said Hamilton. "He'll cut a Suez Canal through to Tanganyika before you can say 'knife'."

"Dear old Ham," said Bones testily, "why jest, dear old boy? I don't profess to be a Lipstic——"

"Lesseps," wailed Hamilton.

"I don't even profess to be dear old thingamejig who built the Pyramids; but a simple surveying job. . . ."

He was amused at the fatuity of asking for outside help.

"You might try to establish contact with Theresa, and if you can, take a couple of men to the village. From what I've heard, she's as ugly as sin and as vain as the devil."

"A typical woman," murmured Bones, and Hamilton restrained himself with great difficulty. "Naughty, naughty! Put down the salt-cellar, dear old Ham," said Bones reproachfully. "Jolly old Excellency and I understand each other quite. What you wish me to do, dear sir and administrator, is to say a few words to this uppish young damsel. I'll talk to her like a father——"

"She'll probably talk to you like a wife," said Hamilton.

He spoke with the voice of prophecy. A day or two afterwards came a canoe, paddled by Eburi warriors, and with them came the courier of Theresa. He made a long speech about nothing, a longer speech about the looking-glass, and wound up:

". . . lord, the chief of our people is a very wise woman, and she knows all things. Now you have two sons, and one of these she will marry——"

Sanders was on his feet; the courier cowered under the blazing blue of his eyes.

"Go back to the chief of the Eburi and say I have nothing here that she may wed, only a rope that has hanged many chiefs, but has never hanged a woman. Also, I have many soldiers with guns which say 'ha ha,' and sharp steel knives; and if I come to her I will make an end of her and her people. The palaver is finished."

The courier had the appearance of one who was rather glad to make his escape.

Bones went away in the *Wigle* with what dignity he could summon; for Hamilton had brought a gramophone down to the quay, and as the *Wigle* started up river the strains of the "Wedding March" came scrappily to his attentive ears. There was nothing but silence left for him—after all, he had grown hoarse from roaring "cad!" through a megaphone; moreover, it had had very little effect upon his skittish superior.

Bones came to the clay bluff, marked out his camp, and sent a peremptory order to K'saga to come and bring with him every able-bodied man of his village. About a hundred responded, old and young, and with the help of these he placed the little camp in a condition of defence; made a rough sort of harbour for the protection of the motor-launch, and mounted his machine-guns at strategical points, covering the hard road which presently lost itself in the marshes.

K'saga's men grumbled and worked. At the end of the first day Bones counted heads and found that at least half of the men had sneaked back to their village. He took six Houssas into K'saga's stronghold, hauled out the two headmen responsible for the recruiting of labour, and flogged them. The next morning the full complement came and stayed till the end of the day.

He had been four or five days established when K'saga came to him with a story of a woman who had been stolen by the Eburi while she was in the forest gathering wood. Bones listened to the circumstantial story without interruption. When K'saga had finished:

"Find this woman and bring her to my camp—and she shall be alive, K'saga, or you will be dead at the breaking of the day."

At midnight they came to him, bringing the woman with them, alive and well; a terrified creature, too frightened to answer questions. Bones beckoned the chief aside.

"Take her back to your village, and if she disappears, you also disappear," he said.

Evidently the appearance of an armed force on the edge of the marsh had impressed the new chieftain of the Eburi. She sent a messenger to guide Bones to her village, but added a significant rider:

"Because it is a great danger, the woman says bring no soldiers, lest they be lost in the marshes."

But Bones bargained for two, and apparently this compromise had been already arranged.

He left at dawn, camped in the forest, sleeping in the fork of a tree, and came to the village in the middle of a scorching day, when men found it hard to work, though the women were lively enough, for they were preparing food for the great festival of M'shimba-M'shamba.

Now, in the bad old days before the law came to the river, the feast of M'shimba-M'shamba was not a nice observance. There were human sacrifices, and the three poles slung in the middle of the village street in triangular form looked rather ominous to Mr. Tibbetts, who had seen several similar tokens of sacrifice.

The attitude of the people was not unfriendly, but rather familiar. They had been so long dissociated from symbols of authority that they were more in awe of the two Houssas, with their loaded rifles and fixed bayonets, than they were of Bones.

There came a councillor to him, a tall stripling, newly recruited from Theresa's dancing boys.

"Tell me, O man, why are these sticks of wood put here?"

The "councillor" answered without hesitation.

"In a day and a day the rime of the moon will come, and we do magic to M'shimba-M'shamba, as our fathers did."

"As your fathers did," repeated Bones gently. "O man, that is a strange saying; for your fathers did evil things: they chopped young girls, tied them to the stake, and watched them burn."

The councillor showed his first sign of uneasiness.

"We of the Eburi are a great people—" he began oratorically, "and what we do is right, for none can come up against us because of the water land——"

Bones opened his mouth wide and scratched his nose, and when he did that he was thinking very quickly.

"What are you, man?" he asked.

"I am a councillor," said the youth proudly; "also I am one of the chief woman's many husbands."

It was towards sunset when he was granted his interview. He found the queen sitting on her stool, and, grouped in a half-circle about her, some twenty young men, each with coloured feathers in his hair. Theresa was rather above middle height. Her face was disfigured with the marks which smallpox leave; she was very skinny and scantily attired. She pointed to the space before her.

"Sit, white man," she said.

Bones stood, towering over her.

"I see you, I'safi-M'lo'bini," he said, and was shocked when she answered in English.

They brought a stool for Bones, and on this he condescended to sit, immediately opposite her—not a favourable position for one who was rather requiring in the matter of duty.

"Now, Tibbetti, you shall tell me stories of wonderful things," she said.

Bones had himself to blame that he had acquired up and down the river the reputation of official story-teller. He had wonderful powers of invention, and had the gift of utilizing the limited vocabulary of the Bomongo tongue to its fullest advantage.

"I'safi," he said, "I will tell you these stories; but first you shall tell me why these sticks stand before your hut." He pointed to the sacrificial poles.

Evidently she had the explanation prepared, for she talked glibly enough, and there was no word of sacrifice.

"That is a good story," said Bones politely, when she had finished. "Now you shall tell me, woman chief, who are the three girls who are kept in little cages on the outskirts of your village?"

Here was a calamitous question. Theresa crossed herself ludicrously, and for a moment forgot her advantage, and was almost humble.

"They will be released," said Bones sternly, "and there will be no killing palaver."

It took the greater part of twenty minutes to free the captives, and by that time Theresa had recovered some of her equanimity. Realizing that his grip of the situation was slipping away, Bones began his story. He could adopt the deep, sonorous tones of the Akasava people, and he told of M'shimba-M'shamba and the fiery lizard whose glance is death, and of the little ghosts who live in the forest, and the devils that come up out of the river and eat dogs; and as he narrated, he saw his breathless audience growing larger and larger with every minute, until he sat in a circle of staring eyes. He allowed his fancy to embroider and invent, and on the spot he created M'pita, the snake god, who lives underground and harms none.

"His skin is white, his eyes are red. Let any man or woman look upon those eyes, and if he is ugly he becomes beautiful; if he is small he grows to be a giant. If it is a woman, then she is so lovely that all the world kneels to her."

It is possible that Bones was instigated by the too obvious plainness of his hostess. It is certain that she listened with growing eagerness, her unshapely mouth opening wider and wider.

"Where is this wonderful ju-ju, Tibbetti?" she asked huskily.

Bones waved his hand airily towards the distant river.

"And have you looked upon him, Tibbetti?"

It was on the tip of Bones' tongue to say that he had a daily conference with M'pita, but remembering the consequence, he modestly confessed he had not.

"But I have seen his trail, like the sheen of gold. Some day I will dig a deep hole and find it for you—if you will obey the laws your father Sandi desires." Bones went back to his camp next morning, well satisfied with himself, and wrote a long and incoherent letter to Sanders. His position was not entirely free from danger. Natives have short memories, and the magic of M'pita might too soon dissolve.

A story came down that the M'shimba sacrifice had been made. The father of the dead girl escaped across the marsh to tell the story. Bones flew a pigeon to headquarters, and he was waiting for the reply, pacing up and down in the wood, watching with a malignant eye the quaking marsh which separated Theresa from retribution, when there came to him the most brilliant idea of his career.

His *lokali* sent a message to the Eburi. The next morning came Theresa's messenger.

"Go to your mistress and tell her that I have found M'pita. Let her send me all the young men of her village, that I may show them where to dig."

That afternoon was one of feverish activity for Bones. He summoned K'saga and his workmen, and made a rough calculation.

"Dig me a deep hole there," he said, and reluctantly they obeyed.

The next morning brought eager recruits to the work. By nightfall a deep channel had been cut through heavy clay, and on the following morning Theresa herself came to watch operations.

"We shall find the snake. I am following his trail," said Bones solemnly.

Working frantically, the men of the Eburi enlarged and extended what was by now something that resembled a railway cutting. They slipped and slithered through the wet clay; they cut down trees that impeded their progress; turned the channel to avoid the rocks; but never once did they see M'pita the snake, whose look brings beauty.

It was towards the close of that day that the watching Theresa made a discovery.

"O Tibbetti, you are making a new river!"

Already the men in the cutting were working knee-deep in water. Bones leaned wearily against a clay bank and grinned feebly. He was on the point of collapse. All day he had been flying hither and thither with the restless energy of an ant. He had marked the progress of M'pita with sticks driven into the ground; he had produced from the *Wiggle* a theodolite, the functions of which he imperfectly understood, and he had abandoned this for a more rough and ready method.

"He carries a little red book which is full of magic," one of the youthful councillors reported.

By sunset the waters from the marsh had piled waist-high at the head of the cutting. With the aid of fires the work went on through the night.

K'saga took counsel with a familiar.

"It is dark, and Tibbetti cannot see. Let all our people steal away to the village and sleep."

Bones did not notice the disappearance of the outcasts until he looked around for one of K'saga's men, certain doubts having arisen in his mind.

Two hours before dawn he blew up the last obstacle that separated his new river from the lower ground. . . .

Theresa came to him in the early light of day, and there was consternation in her face.

"Lord, my young men say that the water is running from my beautiful waterland, and that soon one will walk dryly where the terrible mud would have swallowed them. And all this has happened because they dug up the earth seeking M'pita, the white snake."

Bones had his escort ready—sixteen men with loaded rifles, and two at each machine-gun.

"Go back to your village, woman," he said. "Soon Sandi will come, walking freely where the waters were, and he will bring judgment."

He wrote a letter to headquarters and sent it by a fast canoe.

"SIR AND EXELENCY EXERLENCY,"

"*Vini Veritas Vide Vice!* I have have found it! The serlution of mitilery military dificulties in re Eburi. I have draned the bason! I have draind the basun! Vini vici etc. The whole of the marsh as per sch— sced— schudle in margin is slowly drayning itself to pieces! By cuting cutting a X section through the clay and carefuly studing the contoors contuours different heights of the land I succeded in finding an outlet for the waters. Pro boni publici!"

"Why this strange rush of Latin?" asked Sanders.

There could be only one explanation.

"Bones is under the impression that Lipstick was a Roman."

Sanders was studying a big-scale map of the Eburi.

"A great idea of Bones'—a marvellous idea. I wonder where the dickens he got his labour?"

Hamilton was looking over his shoulder.

"Where the dickens does the water find its outlet?" he asked. "It couldn't run into the river direct."

56

K'saga could have supplied an answer were he alive, for where his unsavoury village had been there had appeared a new lake, beneath whose placid surface was hidden much that were better hidden. And in this lake the crocodiles and water snakes that the draining marsh had left homeless were finding new lairs.

VII

THE SPLENDID THINGS

THE TWO Splendid Things which the people of the Inner N'gombi prized above all other communal possessions were kept in a secret place under a great stone in the bed of a river. Not a great river, because the N'gombi folk have an antipathy to water that runs in any volume.

Literally they were called the very-great-and-beautiful-long-bright-dividers-of-life, but only certain initiated witch doctors and wise men who dabbled in magic gave them their full title. For the common people they were K'sara-K'sura, "The Splendid Things." And after they had been dug up and nastily employed (as they were at times without the knowledge or approval of Mr. Commissioner Sanders) they were wiped clean and polished and laid in an oblong mould of clay into which the juices of a certain tree had been poured. More liquid was poured upon them until they disappeared in the heart of a great block of red rubber. Then they would be replaced and hidden in the river until they were again brought forth.

The Anthropological Commission which the United States Government sent to Africa came in course of time to the River Territory. It consisted of three wise men of middle age and genial disposition. They were, in truth, never wholly deserving of the curses which were poured forth upon their unoffending heads, not only by Mr. Sanders, but by the Administrator, the Colonial Secretary in London and his colleagues of the Cabinet.

On the other hand, the wrath and indignation of certain American newspapers and that section of the scientific American public interested in anthropology, was wholly misdirected and unjust. For Sanders and the British Government were alike innocent of any intention to deceive the great scientists of the United States or to withhold from them information to which they were entitled.

As to Lieutenant Tibbetts of the King's Houssas, the last thing in the world he desired was the publicity that came his way. The night the Commission came down river in the *Zaire* with a miscellaneous collection of spears, arrows, native manufactures, and volumes of data ranging from tribal face marks to cranial measurements, Sanders entertained the scientists to dinner. And it was quite a cheery function, for these men of science were very human, had a fund of good stories, and one at least was a passable tenor.

When the hilarity had died down. . . .

"Bones, of course, was invaluable," said Dr. Wade, the leader of the American expedition. "His facts were a little distorted but his imagination was amazing!"

"Be just, dear old transatlantic cousin!" protested Bones. "Be fair, dear old George Washington! Who showed you the village of the bald men? Who showed you the identical spot where the jolly old green crocodile lays his naughty old eggs? Who, at the risk of his jolly old life, led you into the bushman's dark and sinister lair, where the foot of white man, dear old professor, never, or seldom, trod?"

"You did"—Dr. Wade puffed at his pipe—"through the vilest forest path we have ever struck. We were two days and nights on the journey. We could have made it on the *Zaire* in six hours—and in comfort."

Bones was unabashed.

"You wouldn't have had the experience, dear old anthro—whatever the word is," he said calmly.

"And as to the green crocodile—there is no green crocodile," Wade went on remorselessly, his eyes twinkling behind thick lenses, "and we spent three days looking for the fool thing!"

"Sir and brother scientist," said Bones solemnly, "I've seen it with my jolly old peepers."

Captain Hamilton of the Houssas snorted.

"Yes, you did! A year ago the river people captured an unfortunate croc and painted him green for your benefit."

Bones shrugged his shoulders rapidly.

"He gave us one bit of information which unfortunately came to nothing," said Dr. Wade. "Or shall I say that we could not induce the people of the Inner N'gombi to oblige us."

"What was that?" asked Sanders curiously.

"We tried to get a specimen of the Splendid Things."

Bones closed his eyes patiently.

"If you'd only left it to me, dear old Uncle Sam—" he murmured. "Tact, dear old sir—finesse, jolly old investigator——"

"The truth is, I suppose, that that was another of Bones' dreams?" suggested the burly Mr. Halliman Steel, second in command of the expedition.

Sanders shook his head.

"Ah!" said Bones triumphantly. "My jolly old honour an' veracity is vindicated. Sir an' Excellency. I thank you."

He jerked out a bony hand to Sanders.

"Bones was right." Sanders touched the extended fist with his finger-tips in the manner of the Ochori. "I myself have never seen the Splendid Things, though I have searched for them—naturally. One doesn't allow a couple of business-like execution knives to be floating round without making an attempt to find them. I more than suspect that the Inner N'gombi people use them at rare intervals to slice off the heads of objectionable people, but I've never caught them at it. Some day I will have a bit of luck. I promise you that if ever a specimen falls into my hands—and they are, I believe, unique—I will send it along to you."

The expedition left next day and Bones accompanied the party to Administrative Headquarters.

Now, as everybody knows, His Excellency Sir Macalister Campbell had a daughter more beautiful than any Administrator's daughter had ever been within living memory. Her name was Doran, and Bones was her slave.

When he had handed over his charges to the proper officials he went in search of the divinity and met her coming back from tennis.

"It is quite unnecessary to run and wholly undignified to whoop when you see me," she said severely. "You must remember, Bones, that I am not a child any longer."

She was in the region of eighteen. They had not met for six months, and six months is an awful long time when you are eighteen.

"Dear old Miss Doran . . . simply wonderful . . . bless your jolly old eyes. . . ." Bones was a little incoherent—most elaborately relieved her of her racket and shoes, all of which he dropped from time to time between the place of meeting and her destination.

She had been to England; was (she told him this in their first few minutes of their reunion) half-engaged to a handsome man of great fortune. She was not a child any longer (she told the miserable young man this three times) but she was awfully glad to see her old friends again.

"I suppose you have quite forgotten me—such is the loyalty of one's friends!"

Bones dropped racket and shoes to hammer home his passionate argument.

"Dear old Doran, have a heart—you go home an' get half-engaged to a jolly old he-vamp an' talk to poor old Bones about loyalty. An' here was I thinkin' about you, dear old Doran, in the jolly old lonely watches of the night, dear old miss! 'What's she doin' now?' an' all that sort of stuff——"

"Don't bully me, Bones—I am a woman, I am no longer a child," said Doran.

"Compared with me," said Bones fiercely, "you're a jolly old squeaker!"

"I think you have gone far enough," Doran's voice was like the tinkle of ice against steel.

She was more gracious at dinner. Whilst Sir Macalister was initiating the American commission into the mystery of bagpipes, Bones led her out on to the cool, dark stoep, but the speech he had rehearsed, and which was to reveal his deep contrition and proper humility, was never delivered in its entirety.

"Dear old Miss Doran," he began, "I am but a rough but jolly old soldier, rude of speech——"

"Very rude," she said. "You must remember, Bones——"

"I know you're not, young miss. As I was sayin'——"

"What *are* the Splendid Things?" she asked. "Or was it one of your tarradiddles?"

Bones choked in his righteous indignation.

"Tarradiddles, young Miss Excellency? Bless my jolly old soul! Could old Bones lie?"

"Yes," she said, all too promptly. "But honestly, Bones, are these awful things in existence?"

"They are," said Bones.

"Then get one for me," she said calmly.

The request momentarily deprived him of speech.

"There's nothing in the world——" he began.

"You told that nice American man at dinner that if he had left it to you, the knives would have been in his kitbag—those were your very words."

"What I meant——"

"Get one for me." Her lips curled. "It *was* a tarradiddle."

Bones rose from the wicker chair. He was very stiff and regimental.

"The knife or knives will be in your hands or hand on or before the fourteenth ult.," he said sternly. "It may mean, dear old Miss Hard-heart, that poor old Bones will not be alive to deliver same as per your jolly old orders; it may be that in some lonely, as it were, fever-ridden an' simply fearful land, his mangled old body——"

"Send them by post," said Doran; "and register them."

Bones bowed slightly.

"Wrapped in white paper or blue, young miss?"

"Don't be silly, Bones. You seem to forget that I am no longer——"

Bones laughed harshly and insultingly.

He had been back at Sanders' headquarters a week before his opportunity came.

B'firi, a little chief of the Inner N'gombi, had some trouble with his third and youngest wife. She had reached the summit of ambition in that four men loved her, for she was, by the standards of the forest, very beautiful. Now such a palaver is a great jest amongst hunters when they meet over their cooking pots in the deeps of the N'gombi forest, and it is food for mirth amongst all women wherever they meet; but the wife of B'firi loved best an Akasava fisherman who dwelt in solitude on the banks of the river. M'Lini (this was the name of the beautiful wife) fell into error. For the Akasava are fish-eaters. And fish-eaters are abominable people.

M'Lini was haled before the council of the village, and certain prying men and women gave evidence, with minute details of all they had seen or heard. The palaver lasted through the night, and the stranger who presided, and who, despite the camwood that disguised his face, everybody knew to be B'mingo B'guri, the paramount chief of the Inner N'gombi, ordered her for judgment.

In the deeps of the forest, the keeper of the Splendid Things brought his treasures; the rubber was hacked away from them. . . .

Thereafter M'Lini was not. Nor the lonely Akasava fisherman. These two they buried feet to feet, and the knives were cleaned and polished, soaked again in liquid rubber and hidden in their secret place.

Sanders had the vaguest news of the happening, the merest hint of a hint, the rumour of a rumour; but it was enough to send Bones and ten Houssas on a tour of investigation, and Bones accepted the opportunity as an especial act of Providence arranged for his sole benefit.

"The knives haven't been out for eight years," said Sanders at parting. "Find them and bring them down. If B'firi is implicated in the business beyond a doubt —hang him. But get the knives. I should like to send one to those Americans."

Bones had a use for the other.

For three weeks he trudged to and fro in the Inner N'gombi forest. He held palavers, he examined chiefs and petty chiefs, he inspected the lonely fisherman's hut, and probed and dug in likely spots for evidence of the crime.

"Lord, it is true that my woman has left me," said B'firi. "She left one dark night when the river was so and the moon was so, with an evil man of the Akasava, an eater of fish, who has his hut in such a place. . . ."

Now it is true that even in the N'gombi forest, women run away from their husbands, and here they bear a curious resemblance to their European sisters; they choose as companions in their adventures the most unlikeable people. For who can gauge the curious workings of a woman's mind, whether she be white or brown, fine lady of Mayfair or half-naked wife to a little chief?

There were three brothers of the Akasava who loved one another. In their youth they joined hands together and swore by salt and goats and women that they would bear each other's afflictions, and make wrong done to one the hurt of all three. And though they separated and each became a lonely fisherman their oath held.

It was one of these men who died for his fancy, and even whilst Bones was toiling and moiling in a forest that was as hot as the average Turkish bath, one of the brethren took his canoe and searched out his fellow.

"N'kema is dead," he said. "Because he took the woman of B'firi of the N'gombi, these men have taken out their secret knives and chopped him."

"That is bad palaver," said M'laka, who was the elder brother; "for it seems that these secret knives have a great magic, and up and down the river they say that the man who slays with the Splendid Things may only die from its edge. Let us go into the N'gombi forest and ask questions of the people."

"They may chop us," said the younger brother, but M'laka nodded—thus do the Akasava express dissent.

"Tibbetti is in the forest, seeking the knives, and they will not hurt us because they are afraid."

So the two men polished their spears with river sand, and made their edges very sharp by rubbing them one against the other, and when these things were done they went downstream in one canoe, landed at the edge of the N'gombi forest, and began their investigations. Once they were in the village where Bones was conducting his own enquiries, but he never knew this.

A week after he had gone, M'laka made a discovery.

"The Keeper of the Splendid Things is B'firi himself," he said gravely.

They were sitting over a small fire, roasting a monkey, when the revelation was made.

"It was this B'firi," he went on, "who struck off our brother's head. Now it seems to me that B'firi will talk to us and tell us his mystery. He goes often to the forest to hunt monkeys and often he goes alone. He is quick with the spear, but are we not wonderful stabbers of fish? We will make a fish of him, but he must not die until he speaks."

For a week they haunted the outskirts of B'firi's village, living in holes in the ground so that none could see them, and on the eighth day came B'firi alone, and him they trailed for a mile till, as he stooped to pull an arrow from a wriggling monkey, they leapt at him. Swift to turn and swift to strike, B'firi fought back. His killing spear sent the younger brother to the ground, but M'laka caught and choked him into insensibility.

"I am dead," said the younger brother, and anticipated the truth by a quarter of an hour.

With a rope in his mouth and his hands tied, B'firi watched the burying. Not a word said M'laka until he had brought his captive to the edge of the river.

"I cannot kill you because of your magic," he said.

"That is true," answered B'firi, "for only the Splendid Things can make a ghost of me, and if you try to spear me, you will be turned into a fish."

"That I know," said M'laka. "Now you shall tell me where you hide your bright knives."

B'firi showed his teeth at this.

He showed more of them later when M'laka made a hot fire and burnt his feet a little.

"They are beneath a stone near the Three Teeth of M'shimba-M'shamba," he groaned.

M'laka went alone, since his enemy was in no state for walking, and near the three grey trees which the lightning had withered, he found the stone in the shallow of the river and brought back the knives in their resilient packing.

"If you kill me, Sandi will hang you on a high tree," said B'firi, "but if you take the knives to him he will give you a great reward."

"If I hang, you die, and what greater reward can Sandi give me than my life?" demanded M'laka, and struck.

Bones came down to Headquarters, baffled but not entirely hopeless. His report quite satisfied the Commissioner. He had not expected that the matter would be cleared up so easily. But would it satisfy Miss Doran Campbell? Bones found a letter waiting from her, and read it with many tut-tuts and sundry clucking noises of irritation.

> "DERE BONES," (Doran and Lieutenant Tibbetts had this much in common, that neither could spell) "Have you forgoten your promus? Is it a case of out of site out of mined? I have not forgoten. Remember I am a child no longer!! A promus is a promas. I have prackterly promissed the knifes to a friend of mine in Scotland. Do not dissipoint me, Bones."

Bones sighed heavily and cursed the loquacity of Dr. Wade. He had begun a letter, which was at once tactful and cunning, when there blew into the territory *H.M.S. Tiny*. *H.M.S. Tiny* is an ugly ship, smaller than the average pleasure steamer, and that it should be in salt water at all was something of a novelty, for *Tiny's* duty was to patrol certain small rivers in another British possession, and to check the nefarious traffic in synthetic rum, which certain evil-minded traders pursued contrary to the law. She was in fact on her way, in response to the frenzied demands of an official a thousand miles along the coast line, when something went wrong with her boilers and she wallowed into the river for repairs.

Her ship's company was mainly made up of Kroo-boys, but there were five white officers, and for a week Headquarters was a place of unusual hilarity. The day before she sailed, Bones went on board to tiffin, and was shown round the ship.

"There isn't another boat like this in the world," said Widgeon, her captain, who had a pride that was almost pathetic.

"Dear old naval officer, why should there be?" asked Bones, and advanced the novel theory that the *Tiny* had once been a barnacle on a battleship.

"She can do nine knots," said the indignant officer.

Bones could afford to smile.

"Ever been on the *Zaire*, dear old shipmate?" he asked.

"The *Zaire*? Do you mean that row-boat with the chimney-stacks?" demanded the captain.

Bones quivered.

"She can do twelve knots, old thing—fourteen when I'm in charge of her."

"Wake up," said the captain of the *Tiny* insultingly.

There they might have parted, but the conversation occurred in the boiler room, and Bones' eye was attracted to a bundle of curiously shaped instruments. They had wooden handles and long, jagged blades. In appearance they might well have been mistaken for two-sided saws. Bones pulled one from the bundle and examined it curiously.

"That's a boiler knife," explained the captain shortly. "We use them to clean out the boilers. They'd be too big for the *Zaire*—she wants pen-knives!"

Bones gasped as there came to him the recollection of his promise. Nothing so ferocious as these boiler cleaners had ever been seen in the Territory.

"Dear old Nelson," he said agitatedly, "forget all the perfectly awful things I've said about your perfectly awful ship; accept my apologies, dear old Paul Jones, but could you, *could you* let me have a couple of these jolly old scrapers?"

"You can have the lot," said the captain magnificently. After all he hadn't to pay for them.

Bones went ashore with the two fearsome weapons tucked under his arms, and spent the evening in his hut, covering the blades with varnish and the handles with a bright design in red, green and yellow paint.

By the mail steamer which called at Administrative Headquarters a week later, there arrived a long parcel and a long but dignified letter.

"DEAR YOUNG MISS DORAN, Excelsior! In other words, I have found them I have found them. It was a terible business teribble business. I will not tell you of my adventures my jolly old aventures facing fearful hordes odds. I will not tell you, dear old skeptic, of the dangers through which I pased passed. No, young miss, it is not for old Bones to blow his own trumpit. But what do I care for danjir dannger. . . ."

There was a great deal more in this strain.

"How perfectly wonderful!" breathed Miss Doran Campbell as she examined, with a delicious shudder, the terrifying presents that the mail had brought.

The matter should have ended with her ecstatic letter of thanks, which Bones carried in the pocket nearest to his heart for the greater part of a month. Or it might as well have ended with the receipt by an enthusiastic collector in Scotland of two boiler knives, which later appeared in a glass case inscribed "Execution knives from Central N'gombi tribe. Very rare." Unfortunately, the collector was also a writer. He penned an article in a local newspaper. A reader of the local newspaper had a son who was occupying a position on an important New York journal. In course of time the Sunday edition of this newspaper came out with a whole page showing the map of Africa, sprinkled with photographs of natives, and a large picture, extending across the page, of the two knives. There was also a heading:

> "What the U.S. Anthropological Commission Missed!
> Mystery Knives of Lost Tribe find their
> way to Scottish Museum."

Dr. Wade, leader of the anthropological commission, was not unnaturally annoyed. He wrote a long article in a scientific journal, giving a faithful account of how he had sought for these knives. It needed but this to stir the wrath and indignation of the scientific and lay press. A Chicago newspaper appeared with a splash heading.

"U.S. Scientific Mission Fooled by British Official . ."

The Secretary of State wrote to the British Ambassador a private letter, in the course of which:

> ". . . it is rather unfortunate that this has happened. Wade tells me that he made every effort to get these knives, and seemingly they were available. In fact, either Mr. Sanders or Sir Macalister Campbell must have had them in their possession all the time. I wish you would look into this. The Institute people are rather annoyed. . . ."

The British Ambassador thought the matter of sufficient interest to cable London. But before this message could be dealt with, an echo of the ruffled American press had reached Parliament.

Mr. Burber (East Notts.) asked the Colonial Secretary whether his attention had been drawn to an extract in that morning's *Daily Megaphone* concerning the discourtesy shown by British officials to a great scientific expedition. Sir John Fenny, Colonial Secretary, replied that the matter had not been brought to his notice, but he would cause enquiries to be made. That evening a long message went forward to Sir Macalister Campbell.

Sir Macalister had no time to reply, when two London newspapers, not exactly friendly to the Government, had taken up the cause of the Commissioner.

> "Whilst we have every desire to further scientific research," said the *Daily Post*, "and to pay the tribute due to American enterprise, is not our first duty to ourselves? We are paying the United States an enormous sum per annum in the reduction of our debt. Surely it is a little unreasonable that the United States should object to our retention of historical treasures discovered in British territory. . . ."

In the meantime:

"The curious thing about me, Ham, old boy," said Bones complacently, as he lay stretched on a chair on the stoep and watched four Houssa defaulters drilling under the watchful eye of a sergeant, "is that wherever I go, dear old sir and officer, I'm popular. Popularity seems to come natural to some people."

"Did you ever know a clown that was unpopular?" snarled Hamilton, in the convalescent stage of a fever bout.

Bones could afford to smile.

"Not being so well acquainted with jolly old circus tumblers as you, Ham, I can't tell you. But it's a funny thing that from the Administrator down to you——"

"You're not popular with me; get that delusion out of your diseased mind," said Hamilton.

"Look at dear old Excellency Campbell! Look at jolly little Miss Doran! Look at your own revered and beloved Excellency! For me?" He rose to meet the telegraph operator.

"No, sah, for the Commissioner."

It was a long telegram, Sanders noted, as, groaning, he took the message in his hand. Hamilton saw his face drop.

"Trouble, sir?" he asked.

"More work for poor old Bones," murmured that young man. "It's a very funny thing about me——"

"Everything's funny about you," snapped Hamilton.

And then Sanders' voice broke in.

"What on earth is all this about? Listen:

"Very urgent. Report immediately how N'gombi execution knives came into your possession, whether they were in your possession when American scientific expedition here, circumstances of discovering them. Request special report from Lieutenant Tibbetts giving name of village, custodian and other particulars. This information required by Government without delay. Acknowledge."

"Execution knives?" said Sanders. "They mean the Splendid Things, I suppose. But you didn't find them, did you, Bones?"

Bones was blinking rapidly; his mouth was open but only strange sounds issued.

"The fact is, dear old Excellency——" he said hoarsely.

"Did you find them or didn't you?" asked Hamilton.

"The truth is, dear old sir and Commander-in-Chief——"

"Oh, you——"

"Dear old officer, was I to blame?" said Bones rapidly, almost tearfully. "Here's a jolly old young miss . . . word of honour, dear old officer . . . I promised her, dear old Ham . . . a gentleman . . . a lady . . . gracious heavens alive, dear old sir, my jolly old honour was at stake!"

"Even if it had been something important, you had no right to deceive the girl," said Hamilton severely. "I think that lets us out, sir."

But Sanders was not looking at him; his eyes were fixed upon the man who had been escorted across the square by the sergeant of the guard and who now stood before the Residency steps, a bundle in his arms.

"I see you, Sandi," boomed the stranger. "I am M'laka of the Akasava, and I have come many days in my little boat to bring you a wonderful present which Tibbetti your son has sought."

He unrolled the native cloth which covered the knives he carried.

"Here, lord, is the magic of the Inner N'gombi people, for I have found the Splendid Things which destroyed my brother."

Sanders stared down at the execution knives curiously worked and terribly sharp, and he saw that one was stained brown, and guessed that stain for the blood of B'firi, the headman. . . . . . .

There came to Bones a letter from Administrative Headquarters, and for a long time he had not the courage to open it:

"DERE MR. BONES"—the letter began, severely enough—"I reely am supprised at you. You've made me look a perfect fool!!! Papa has sent on the real execution knife to America, and I've had to rite to Scotland to get back that wretched, wretched boiler knife. After this our corrispondince must cease. You have treated me abomminably. You seem to forget I am no longer a child."

"Yours truly,"
"DORAN CAMPBELL."

"P.S. Couldn't you get me the other real knife? Do be a darling and try."

MISS CAROLINE TIBBETTS was a lady of amazing character. She was one of three sisters and brothers, and no one knew the extent of her wealth. The very uncertainty in this respect was her charm and her attraction to a dozen distant relatives, all of whom hoped that, whatever else happened, her nephew Augustus would do something terrible in Aunt Caroline's eyes, to leave the way open for a fair distribution of property amongst those who had less claim to it. For she was notoriously touchy and staid, was a Baptist in good standing, a supporter of missions sent out by that admirable sect, and intolerant of all who yielded to the temptations which had never come her way.

Bones wrote to her regularly, not because he wanted her money, but for fear that she might think that he didn't.

"Augustus is a very good lad," she said to a needy relation who was staying with her at Chichester.

The relative sighed.

"Young men—one never knows what they are up to," she said, "especially in a lawless country where—um—if one can believe the missionary journals, licence is unbridled."

Miss Tibbetts, who was thin, sharp-featured and rather short, sniffed. She had reason for sniffing, for she, also, had read the interesting report in *Light in Darkness*—a journal published by the Bomongo Mission.

There had been a minor scandal in a certain state that had been magnified into a major scandal. A certain inspector of police—but why drag up the unamusing details?

Miss Tibbetts was planning her winter holiday, and had decided upon Madeira. The great idea came to her one afternoon in the Bay of Biscay, after a little talk with the purser, who was bemoaning the poverty of the passenger list and the good accommodation that went begging.

"By the time we get to the coast the ship will be empty. We lose half our passengers at Funchal. And it's a lovely trip, Miss Tibbetts—and you've got a nephew on the coast, you tell me? Well, well, well! We could drop you and pick you up on the homeward trip, and you could finish your holiday at Madeira. Fever? Good gracious, no! It's as safe as Clapham. And you'd only be there a week."

Miss Tibbetts thought this over. Such of his letters as she could decipher filled her with an uneasiness about the spiritual welfare of Augustus.

She discussed the matter with her companion, the middle-aged lady in reduced circumstances who was privileged to call her Caroline, being a distant cousin. And Mrs. Crewfer jumped at the suggestion.

"I haven't seen Augustus for years," said Miss Tibbetts.

Mrs. Crewfer sighed.

"I hope he's going on the right way," she said, in a tone that revealed her confident belief that he wasn't.

"My money will make no difference to him one way or the other," said Miss Tibbetts, "but I'd like to be sure that it is going to the right person."

Mrs. Crewfer shook her head.

"I hope so," she said, which was not true.

She might have foreseen the complications that were already arising over a certain B'lana.

Because the N'gombi are a forest folk who seldom see the river as children, they do not swim, and drown rather easily. Lieutenant Tibbetts once dived from the bridge of the *Zaire* into a stream running at six knots, and thick with crocodiles, to rescue a girl of the N'gombi named B'lana. It was an act so dangerous and so gallant that Mr. Commissioner Sanders would have recommended him for the Humane Society's Medal if a terrified Bones had not begged him, almost with tears, not to do any such thing.

"Bones is the queerest bird in the world," said the wondering Hamilton. "You'd never think that one so blatantly immodest would kick up such a fuss."

Sanders smiled.

"Bones is a type. They are immodest about virtues they do not possess, and diffident when it comes to the recognition of their real qualities. If I had offered Bones election to a Fellowship of the Psychical Society, he would have leapt at it!"

Hamilton tossed aside the month-old newspaper he had been reading.

"Do you think Bones *is* psychic?" he demanded.

Sanders took his cheroot from his mouth and stared at the Houssa captain in astonishment.

"What on earth do you mean?" he said, startled.

But Hamilton was very serious.

"It's a queer fact, and you can verify it, but Bones always seems drawn at odd moments to some hobby which has a bearing upon a subsequent experience. It is as though he had a subconscious warning that the adventure was coming. If he takes up the study of anything—musical instruments, architecture, law, history, whatever it is, I am absolutely convinced it is in preparation for some new angle of life that is coming to him."

He gave instance after instance, and Sanders listened thoughtfully.

"His present psychic phase was a little trying," he said, "but if it is in preparation for a personal experience I am not very happy about it."

Mr. Tibbetts was at the moment a student of astral phenomena.

"Dear old Ham," he said, when his superior remonstrated that night after dinner, "you don't understand, old boy. I've always been physic——"

"If you'd only call the dam' thing by its proper name I'd forgive you a lot," said Hamilton, wearily. "P-s-y-c-h-i-c—pronounced 'si-kik.' "

Bones smiled with great tolerance.

"Physic is the word, Ham, old lad; don't tell me, dear old officer, that I don't understand what I am. I was talking to Millie last night——"

"Who?" asked the startled Hamilton.

"Millie—we sat talkin' in my hut for hours. She used to be a friend of King Charles, dear old Ham—but a very respectable young woman, fearfully lady-like."

Hamilton gaped at him in alarm.

"You—Millie . . . a girl?"

Bones nodded gravely.

"She's my familiar, old boy—nothing familiar about her—fearfully how-d'you-do sort of person. . . ."

A light dawned on Hamilton.

"Do you mean she's a spirit?"

Bones nodded.

"How do spirits sit down?" demanded the sarcastic Hamilton. "Did she have a drink by any chance?"

Bones sighed.

"You're a septic, old boy—I can't talk to septics. Now, a physic's never septic."

Hamilton agreed.

"As a matter of fact, we got in touch with an aunt of yours—begins with 'M'."

"Matilda?" suggested Hamilton, and Bones' long face lit up.

"That's right, old boy. Your aunt Matilda. She sent a message for you, old boy. She's terribly happy over there."

"Over where?"

Bones pointed.

"Good lord!" said Hamilton, innocently. "Is she in the guard room?"

Bones was pained.

"Sacred subject, dear old officer—I'm talking about the jolly astral plane . . . where dear old souls go when they pop off."

Hamilton considered this.

"And she's happy?"

"Terribly. She said she's met all the best people, old boy. Jolly old Shakespeare and the tennis man—the johnny who wrote *Called to the Bar*, and all that sort of muck. She's in heaven, dear old fellow."

Hamilton nodded.

"I'm glad—I had a letter from her last mail, and she was in Surbiton then."

Bones was very annoyed.

"Not the game, old officer and septic . . . leadin' me on . . . you told me your Aunt Matilda was dead, an' naturally I didn't doubt her word . . . lady an' all that sort of thing. You said last Christmas Day 'The old thing's buried.'"

"I didn't!" denied Hamilton hotly. "I said she'd gone to live in Surbiton."

"It's the same thing," snorted Bones.

He heard voices at night and made a record of the conversations. Hamilton heard them and raised Cain with the sergeant of the guard for permitting his sentries to grow talkative in the middle of the night. Bones protested the unearthly nature of the voices; he was supported by the sergeant of the guard, dazed and happy to find such support.

One day . . .

"Something has got to be done about Bones," said Hamilton. "He's throwing trances—last night his spirit went to England without so much as my leave."

It was B'lana of the N'gombi who really made ghosts and spirits unpopular . . .

The people of the riverside villages heard the thresh of the *Zaire's* stern wheel and moved uneasily in their beds, for the *Zaire* did not dare the shoals and sandbanks of the great river by night unless there was trouble; and when they heard a loud and raucous voice singing in the darkness the song of the fishermen they shuddered, for none but ghosts sing at night, though the lanky young vocalist was tangible enough.

A watchman on the beach of the Ochori city saw the *Zaire* coming into sight, its twin funnels belching masses of sparks, and, seeing, he strode swiftly to the hut where Bosambo sat, very wakeful and alert.

"Lord, he comes," said he.

"I have ears," answered Bosambo curtly.

He had heard the wheel of the *Zaire* for nearly two hours before she came into sight. Here the river runs swiftly and progress is slow, and ten miles is no great distance for a sound to carry on a quiet, windless night.

The boat swung broadside to the beach, a dozen men scrambled overboard, wading through the river with hawsers on their shoulders, and with the gangplanks fixed came Lieutenant Tibbetts, who had slept all the afternoon, and in any circumstances was never so bright as he was at two o'clock in the morning.

"I see you, Tibbetti," Bosambo's voice boomed from the darkness.

Bones made his polite reply, and together they walked side by side up the dark path to the village. Not until they were inside a big hut, illuminated by a tall lamp which bore a suspicious resemblance to one lost from the *Zaire* on her last visit, did Bosambo speak, and with unusual gravity.

"Lord," he said, "this is a bad palaver. The N'gombi folk, it seems, have gone mad, and my young men have fought two battles with them to-day on the edge of the little river. And all for the matter of a small ghost such as I would not have in my city."

Now the Inner N'gombi folk are peculiar in this, that, whilst they admit the potency of M'shimba-M'shamba, in common with all the people of the river, and offer to him the respect which is due to a devil who appears with thunder and lightning and great words to tear up the trees and level the stoutest of villages, they have, from the beginning of time, elected and appointed their own supreme devil who is master of all other devils and greater.

His name is Dhar, and such a name is not to be spoken aloud, but whispered into a little hole dug in the ground, for Dhar is the devil of earth and heaven, arbiter of fate, giver of life and supreme spirit of death. Dhar brings the seasons and supports in his two hands the sun and the moon, and his eyes are the stars and the hairs of his head are the lesser ghosts and devils.

Since the Inner N'gombi are a proud and warlike people, very sensitive to slight and very quick to avenge an affront, it was a little embarrassing to officials and neighbours alike that the exact manifestation of Dhar was invariably a mystery. Dhar could be as easily a man or woman, a rock—something animate or inanimate. Once, *cala cala*, which means long ago, he was a monkey kept in a large cage in the forest, and fed daintily. Always Dhar is guarded by three maidens of the tribe. Night and day one sits in rapt contemplation of his splendours.

"Lord, how did my young men know that these infidels had chosen a tree?" pleaded Bosambo.

"How did your young men hunt in the forests of the N'gombi?" asked Bones sternly. "Is it not forbidden that the Ochori should take their spears beyond the little river?"

Bosambo very tactfully offered no explanation as to this. The N'gombi forest abounds in game—the adjacent Ochori territory is notoriously bare.

"And coming to this place, they saw a dead tree and cut it down for their fires," Bosambo went on rapidly. "Now, lord, trees are trees, and only heathen men give them souls——"

"O Bosambo," said Bones quietly, "did not the blessed Prophet, in the year of the Hegira, speak with a tree and cause it to be buried as a true believer? And if Mahomet did this, who are you to say that the N'gombi people are infidels?"

Bosambo floundered.

"But this tree was dead——" he began.

"So, also, was the tree of Mahomet, for it was a pillar in his mosque," said Bones, who knew his subject rather well.

Bosambo stared at the storm lantern gloomily.

"Now I see that my young men were wrong," he said, but brightened up. "Let me gather a thousand spears in Sandi's name, and I will go down into the N'gombi country and make an end of these idolaters."

"Don't be an ass!" said Bones testily.

"Same like missionary," murmured Bosambo, giving English for English. "I teach um Marki, Luki, Johnni same like. I find um, I smack um, you savvy. These fellers be fool! How ghost can be if no ghost is?"

Bones coughed and returned to the vernacular.

"Ghosts there are, and I understand their palaver," he said. "You talk, Bosambo, of things about which you know nothing. I know my own ghost well, and often he walks abroad. I will speak to the chief of the Inner N'gombi."

"Lord, that may be dangerous," said Bosambo. "It would be better to send your ghost."

Bones looked at him hard, but there was no hint of sarcasm in the chief's eyes.

With four soldiers in attendance he left at dawn the following morning for the battle front, that same creek which Bosambo and his people were forbidden to cross; and here, after an hour's parley, and having overcome the "enemy's" natural suspicion that his visit was a punitive one, he was escorted through a rank of enraged and sullen warriors to the chief's hut.

"Lord, these men of the Ochori have done a terrible thing," said M'songo, the chief, tremulous with anger, yet a little apprehensive as to what might be the outcome of the war he had started. "As you know, Tibbetti, there is in this land a Great One." He put his hand before his mouth, a conventional gesture to all who spoke even obliquely of Dhar. "And this one lived in a fine tree and brought us prosperity for three and three seasons; nobody in our village died, and no hurt came to any. But the huntsmen of Bosambo came and drove away the maidens who guarded him, saying things to them that frightened them. Since our ghost has been destroyed there is death everywhere, and only this morning H'laki the woodman was killed by a tree falling on him, and all the old men and women have died like fish."

Bones listened sympathetically to the long statement of grievance.

"They who came into your land have broken Sandi's law, and they shall be punished. At the rise of the next moon Bosambo, the chief, shall send you twenty skins and three bags of salt, and at the shallow where they crossed the little river I will put up a piece of wood with certain devil marks on it, so that who shall come into your territory without Sandi's word shall be turned into monkeys. This I do in the name of Sandi, who is your father and your mother, and carries your nation in his arms like a little child."

The chief and his councillors were impressed.

"Some have been killed in this war, Tibbetti, for there has been bloodshed."

"Let blood wash blood," quoth Bones. "Bring back your young men from the river and we will have a great palaver in your city."

The chief hesitated. His men were hot for vengeance; but the prospect of a palaver lasting for days, and offering unlimited opportunities for oratory, beloved of the natives, weighed him to the side of law and order. The fighting men were drawn back, and that night Bones sat in the palaver house and heard the first half dozen of forty-five headmen, all of whom had something uncomplimentary to say about Bosambo.

On the third day the weary Bones closed the debate.

"Who shall mourn the seed when it is become a sapling, or the sapling when it is become a tree?" he demanded. "Is the Great One"—he put his hand before his mouth in the conventional fashion—"so small that he cannot escape from six Ochori huntsmen, so weak that he cannot live when his house is burnt? Now I tell you that he lives and wanders in the forest looking for a new home, and this you must find for him as your fathers did. I will leave your wise men to make a great talk—this palaver is finished."

That night, as he slept, he heard a noise at the entrance of his hut and was instantly awake, and, turning, saw a shadow in a moonlit patch.

"Who is there?" he asked.

"Lord, it is I."

It was the soft voice of a woman.

"Dear me!" said Bones, and putting on his overcoat over his pyjamas, went out into the moonlight.

She stood six paces from the hut, tall and slim, a long wand in her hand such as the N'gombi women carry.

"I am B'lana-M'songo, the daughter of the chief," she said. "I am very wise and ghosts speak to me."

"Go back to your bed and to your ghosts," said Bones, bad-humouredly.

"Lord, I am she that you saved from the walking fish."

Bones, who had forgotten his act of heroism, scratched his head.

"All nights and all days I think of you, lord, being a maiden with a wonderful mind, and I speak also to the elder men and they listen to me. This has happened to no woman before. Lord, I was one of the women who guarded the tree when Bosambo's hunters came."

"O woman, this you must tell me when I wake," said the weary Bones, and dismissed one to whom he was as a god.

He came back to headquarters not unpleased with himself, stopping at the Ochori city just long enough to impose a fine, which Bosambo bore, since his unfortunate people would have to pay it.

He made his report to Sanders, not attempting to hide the important part his tact and perspicuity had played.

"Naturally, Excellency, I was in my element, being physic. Mind you, there's a lot to be said for these jolly old barbarians——"

"What is the new ghost?" asked Hamilton.

Bones shrugged his shoulders, and made a clucking noise of disapproval.

"I wish, dear old boy, you'd treat physical subjects physically. Does it matter ——"

"It matters a lot," said Sanders quietly. "I wish, Bones, you would find out, the next time you're up there."

"From your girl friend," suggested Hamilton coarsely, but Sanders was serious.

"If we could only know for sure which and what is Dhar, it would make things rather easy. The N'gombi are getting more and more troublesome, and you never know when some innocent outsider will go barging into their mysteries. About twenty years ago Dhar was a missionary's cat, and one of the Isisi bagged pussy, and there was a war which lasted for the greater part of seven years."

"I'll find out," said the confident Bones.

"Send your soul for a trot," suggested Hamilton, but Bones was superior to such levity.

He was half-way to his hut when he heard a shout, and, looking round, saw Hamilton running towards him.

"Anything wrong, brother officer?"

"That I can't tell you," said Hamilton. "Do you remember a little conversation about my aunt?"

Bones closed his eyes in resignation.

"I only asked you," said Hamilton, "because I've got a bit physic myself. I've had a message from your aunt."

"Has she popped off?" asked Bones, eagerly.

"To be exact," said Hamilton, "she's popped up. She's arriving by the mail this afternoon. We've just had a wire from headquarters."

Bones staggered back.

"Aunt Caroline!" he said hollowly. "Suffering Moses!"

Ordinarily Sanders did not like visitors, but he had two of his rooms at the residency prepared for Miss Tibbetts and her companion, and when she arrived, being gallantly carried ashore by Bones—it was a thousand pities that, having made so courteous an effort, he should have put her down ankle-deep in the surf —she found, if not a hearty, at least a kindly welcome.

"I am rather worried about my nephew, Mr. Sanders. He has been talking quite strangely about certain matters. In fact, I thought he might be suffering from one of those terrible mental aberrations which I understand this climate produces. He asked me if my spirit walked, and whether I had had any manifestations. Would you describe him as a good Baptist, Mr. Sanders?"

"He's a very good fellow," said Sanders, cautiously.

Miss Tibbetts looked at her stony-faced companion.

"As to his—um—morals, Mr. Sanders. It is a delicate subject to discuss, but this is a very dangerous climate, and young men . . ." She glanced at Mrs. Crewfer, who shook her head sadly, and seemed prepared for the worst.

"That question does not arise," said Sanders, a little stiffly. "Your nephew is a gentleman, and that should be quite sufficient answer."

But Miss Tibbetts was not convinced. That night she had a long, and, to Bones, a depressing heart to heart talk with him. Mainly it was her heart that was concerned. Bones listened with ill-simulated interest. She had the haziest ideas of the code which governs men in the Government service. She spoke of *mésalliances* with a freedom that made Bones shudder; she suggested possibilities that made his head swim. And then Mrs. Crewfer took a hand.

"You quite understand that your dear aunt is only talking to you for your good, Mr. Tibbetts. One has heard strange stories——"

"My dear old distant relation and companion to revered aunt," said Bones, stung to annoyance, "all this conversation in front of a young boy is perfectly out of order. You are putting ideas in my head, you are, really! Dash it all, dear old Caroline—jolly old aunt, I mean—those sort of things are not done, dear old lady, they aren't, really! . . . Most fearfully embarrassing——" He broke off incoherently.

It was the very next morning that Bones woke an hour after daybreak, with a consciousness that he was not alone in the room.

"O Ali," he said, not opening his eyes, "bring me——"

And then he opened his eyes. There were three very young ladies sitting on the floor, looking at him with great solemnity. They wore nothing worth speaking about, but each had round her head a large garland of dead flowers—cut flowers die readily on the river.

"O lord I see you!"

They spoke in unison, and each lifted a brown palm in salute.

"What the deuce——!" stammered Bones, speaking English in his agitation.

And then he recognized B'lana.

"O woman, you must not sit in my hut. Who brought you from the N'gombi?"

"I came by the big river," said the girl, her large brown eyes fixed on his. "This woman is the daughter of Shimbiri, and this woman is the daughter of Lababuli the headman."

Half an hour later Hamilton, standing on the stoep of the residency, saw Bones stalking across the square with three ladies in pursuit.

"Perfectly ghastly, old boy. . . . I've been elected Dhar . . . this little person's idea." He indicated the serene B'lana. "Something's got to be done, old boy. If aunty sees these young persons . . . good lord!"

Hamilton looked from Bones to his escort.

"Your aunt left an hour ago: the ship came back a day earlier than was expected." He nodded slowly, communing with himself. "That was why she was so haughty."

"W-why?" Bones was aghast.

"She said she didn't want you wakened: she'd go into your hut and wish you good-bye. Bones, I wouldn't give you fourpence for your legacy."

THE RICH WOMAN

THERE was a gentleman in New York who sold mining stock. The stock was beautiful, being printed in four colours, but the mines were as bad as black and white could describe them. He came to the territories, as one of her annual guests, and as he was well supplied with letters of introduction, this Mr. Liberbaum was well received. He was a nice man with an extensive range of superlatives, and since he was agreeable to his hosts they bore him no grudge, even when, as they discovered three months later, he applied for and received a government concession to dredge the river, for gold.

"Gold!" smiled Sanders, "the only gold in the river is my unfortunate cigarette case—and that would not be there if Bones had not been such a goop."

Bones was so interested by the information that he did not attempt to justify the slight error of judgment—it happened during the conjuring trick that he was giving as they came downstream on the *Zaire*.

"That's curious," said Captain Hamilton thoughtfully, "this fellow Liberbaum started questioning me about some native legend. He said he had heard that there was a mysterious gold mine in the country."

"Perfectly true, dear old officer," said Bones promptly. "I have heard it, too, dear old Ham. Bosambo has heard it——"

"Bosambo has heard anything that he can get money out of," said Sanders sardonically. "Did he try to sell you stock?"

Bones was hurt.

"Of course he has heard it—it is an old-established native yarn!" Sanders scoffed. "Sometimes it is gold—sometimes it is diamonds. Once they had a story that in the N'gombi there was a big hole in the ground, out of which you could draw a cloth ready woven!"

It was a considerable time after, and the visit of Mr. Liberbaum had been forgotten when there arrived an urgent telegram from headquarters.

"Liberbaum selling Stock in New York Gold Dredging Company, states you said river alluvial."

Sanders was sufficiently broken to the ways of official correspondence not to reply, "He is a liar," instead he sent a long and decorous denial, and added his views that there was not sufficient gold in the whole of the river to make a shirt stud of respectable size.

But so far as Bones was concerned, the mischief was done. Since the mention of gold he had devoted himself, with all the enthusiasm and energy of which he was capable, to his new hobby. With a huge pipe clenched between his teeth, and three groaning paddlers, he had been searching the foreshores of the river from its mouth to Lumbiri, and native people came miles to stare awe-stricken, watching the perspiring young man sifting and washing the sand.

"If you found gold you would not know what it looked like," said Hamilton.

Bones smiled pityingly.

"If I come to you, dear old boy, with a couple of hands full of auribilous metal, dear old thing."

" 'Auriferous' is the word you want," said Hamilton, coldly, "and if you came with not only a hand, but your mouth full, and that would hold enough to keep a widow woman in luxury—I should simply hand you over to headquarters for trying to obtain money by a trick!"

Again Bones smiled.

"I can only tell you, dear old septic, that all these johnnies along the river know that there is gold! The naughty old lads keep it dark, naturally, dear old Ham, but I am a bit of an authority, dear old septic——"

"Sceptic," murmured Sanders, lounging in his chair, with his eyes closed.

"Thank you, Excellency," with extravagant gratitude. "What I mean to say is, that for somebody who has got the confidence of the indigenous native, there is a fortune—millions, old Excellency—perhaps billions. I have got a great idea."

Hamilton sat up.

"Hail," he said sardonically, "I knew sooner or later you would get one."

"I have got a great idea," ignoring the interruption, "I am entitled to three weeks' leave," he said this very impressively.

"Well, Bones?" Sanders woke up and opened his eyes. "What is the idea?"

"I shall take a quiet slope through the country," said Bones speaking rapidly. "In fact, Excellency, I am going to put into execution a scheme I have had for years. I am going native."

Hamilton groaned.

"If that means you are going to paint your body with woad, let me tell you there is only one man in the territory who has ever been capable of disguising himself as a native, and that is the Commissioner. You will do nothing of the sort, Bones. It only means that you will go up country and stir up the wretched natives to rebellion, or else get yourself into such a mess that the Commissioner and I will be kept busy for months answering minutes from Headquarters."

To his amazement Sanders did not share his view.

"I have often thought of doing the same," he said. "I have not played native for years, and so long as Bones is not seen about in the daytime he might get away with it. There are one or two matters that I should like information on, and about which our agents tell me nothing—I rather think that our men are watched so closely that they have not a ghost of a chance to get near anything interesting."

Sanders had in his mind, as he confessed later, the activities of the three brothers of the Akasava, who with their women were the sole occupants of a tiny village near the island which is called the Fast Waters, at the seaward mouth of one of the deep ravines through which the waters of the great river pile. The stream spreads out to a mile in width and in the very centre, and a menace to navigation, is this cigar shaped island, which has no inhabitants and for a good reason.

The yellow waters discharging themselves from the gorge run so quickly, and the currents are so treacherous, that no man can be assured that he may either gain or leave at his wish. Sometimes, for no apparent reason, the pace of the river hereabouts quickens from four to seven knots, and the Northern arrowhead of the island is partially submerged, a fate which completely overtakes this strip of land after heavy rain. On the mainland lived these three brothers, who were by profession fishermen, though nobody had ever seen their catch, and it was notorious that they purchased dry fish from the villages up and down the river. And yet they were prosperous—they had their dogs and their goats and one, the chief of them, had as many as five wives.

There were dark stories about them. It was said when a wife tired of her husband, or a man grew resentful of his wife's lover, they came secretly and at night bringing payment in advance for certain acts of providence. Some men had been found drowned with none to say how they came to their end. One fascinating lover, who had brought unhappiness to many homes, was found dead in the forest under a fallen tree. Sanders had made many efforts to trap the assassins, but never once had he succeeded, and the brothers Shiribi flourished.

Less than a week after the consultation and the exposure of Bosambo's great plan a lank native was seen in the light of dawn paddling up the river, keeping to slack waters and avoiding, in a marked fashion, the centres of population.

"If they see you by daylight, your childish camouflage is spotted," said Hamilton who came down to the quay at 2.0 a.m. on a rainy morning to see his subordinate depart.

"Trust Bones," said that confident young man.

"I don't," said Hamilton.

Which was true: he never did.

"And I'll come back with the baffling old secret!" yelled the brown man from the water.

"Shur-rup!"

Hamilton at rare intervals was extremely vulgar.

•   •   •   •   •

There was a woman of the Isisi who differed from all other women because she was the only child of her father, and when he had died he had given to her riches beyond the dreams of common men. Gardens and rich dogs, salt in abundance, rods of brass and twenty skin sacks each full to its sewn mouth with silver coins.

Her wealth multiplied, her fields grew larger, for this slip of a girl had learned the mysteries of trading from her father. Skins and rubber, ivory, alive and dead, accumulated in her storehouse, even Bosambo, Chief of the Ochori, who was not interested in women, came to hear of her and having certain goods for disposal—he usually took a large squeeze of the taxation that he remitted to Sanders—he sent his chief headman to her with an invitation and M'Yari came in the state of a queen, in a new canoe with sixteen paddlers and in place of the thatched house in the stern of the canoe, she had one roofed with cloth.

Bosambo was all for his dignity, nevertheless he went down to the landing place to meet her, and offered her flattery of the most primitive kind.

"I hear you Bosambo," said the maiden, when he had finished. "Now, I am not come to hear of my beauty, but to see your skins and your rubber and all the beautiful things you have stolen from your people."

Bosambo swallowed that. For three hours they chaffered and bargained. She went away with a spare canoe stocked with produce and left the Chief with the unhappy feeling that he had been slightly swindled. It was a brand new experience and rather intriguing.

She came again. He adopted a new tactic. His wife having gone to the high ground with her child, because of the humidity (she was a Kano woman), Bosambo received the rich woman with a banquet and a dance and made violent love to her. She held him at spear's end as the saying goes, took back with her more of his saleable goods, and this time he had no doubt whatever that he had the wrong end of a bad bargain.

"Such a thing had never been since the beginning," said one, "that a woman should be so rich. For women belong to men, just as goats belong, and if they belong to men so do all they have, also. Now one of us shall have her as a wife. We will go to N'mari the wise man and he shall tell us which. And whoever gets her shall divide her riches amongst her relations, a half and a half, a half to her uncles and the half of a half to her uncles' children."

It was an uncle who suggested this: the division was disputed but eventually agreed. So they went to N'mari the wise man who lived in the Isisi forest with his snakes and his birds and strange wild animals that slept under his skin bed at nights. With him lived his grandson, the young man B'laba who was a great hunter and a very sour and covetous man.

And they told the old man what they desired. When they had finished he spoke.

"Go to this young maiden and say, 'We desire you to choose a husband from one of us.' Then you shall go away and kill a young cock by the light of the moon and each shall smear his hands with the blood, and in the morning he whose hands have been cleaned by my magic shall have this woman."

So they went away and told the girl who sat before her hut with her women slaves and she said nothing. But she sent one to spy on them.

In the dim light of the new moon they sacrificed and smeared their hands with blood, and each went to his hut where his immediate relative had a pot of water to wash off the stain, and when they met in the morning it seemed that they were all chosen. And each stood exposed as a trickster by the trickery of his fellow. Yet they went again to the wise man, who knew what brought them.

"Go each of you to a different place. You to the Akasava City, you to the little village by the pool of the Silent Ones . . ." He pointed them out one by one and gave each his destination.

"To-morrow I will perform a great magic and bring this girl to me. And all my little ghosts shall sit around her and she shall not see them. Then at the right time I will make her dance until she falls stiffly, and where her head points that shall be the place where her lover is and she shall get up and go to him."

The uncles and cousins were hardly out of sight before, looking up in his half blind way, the old man thought he saw a woman before him.

"I am M'Yari of M'pusu, and I followed these men into the forest knowing they came to speak to you about me. Tell me what I must do. For I am very rich and I need a husband who will be as my little dog and will eat when I say 'eat.' And these brothers of my mother and sons of them are no more to me than the fish of the river. If any of them take me I will pay the three brothers of the Akasava to follow him into dark places and do with him what is necessary."

At that moment came the old man's grandson.

"Here is a fine man who shall be all that you need," he said.

So the maid of M'pusu looked at him and took him home with her, and when the cousins and the uncles, weary of waiting, returned from where they had gone, they found this man in the rich girl's hut, and it seemed that he was master of her and her wealth. For every night they heard the whistle of his hide whip and the smack of it as it fell. But she never cried nor called upon her kin. One night she took a canoe and four women to paddle her.

M'Yari's canoe came in the darkest hours to the little congregation of huts where the three Akasava brothers lived, and since they did their dealings by night, they were waiting for her on the beach, three cold silent men. They knew she was coming, and she was not surprised, and they knew, for in this land mind speaks to mind in some inexplicable manner that only native folk and the ants understand.

She told them her business very briefly:

"This man must not be killed because of Sandi, and his soldiers, but you must hold him so that he does not come back to me again, and if you beat him a little that will be good."

They palavered by themselves on this and in the end agreed, for they too were anxious not to bring themselves actively into conflict with Sanders.

In the meantime B'laba awoke and when he found his wife had gone out, he was afraid thinking that she had gone to find an Akasava assassin.

He went back to the forest and saw the wise old man.

"Take all she has and hide it in a deep hole in the ground," said N'Mari.

For seven nights B'laba sweated under heavy loads, carrying piece by piece the treasures that his wife had had in a deep hole under the floor of the hut. Salt and rods and skin sacks, their mouths sewn tight and big with silver coins.

On the seventh night as he toiled there came through the dark woods three men of the Akasava. They walked very quietly, none saw their canoe laid at the little forest beach where the crocodiles lay basking on sunny mornings. Each carried three spears between his four fingers and they came upon B'laba as he was stooping to re-lift a load of silver. So that everything was favourable for their enterprise. He gave one little hiccupping groan as he tumbled over—and that and the "plop" of the spear haft as it struck his head were the only sounds that disturbed the night, for the Akasava brothers never spoke at all. They lifted the unconscious man and brought him to the river where a girl was waiting in a canoe and she gave them money to take him away.

They would have gone to the hut of the wise old man in the forest and made an end of him, but she said no to this and they left the matter as it was.

The three brothers drew apart and one said to the others:

"If Sandi comes with his soldiers and hears all that he may hear there will be trouble. Now only this woman can speak against us, so let us take her treasure and hide it on the island where we will keep this man, and we will take her ashore with us."

He said this and other things and his brothers shook their heads which meant agreement.

"Also if this man is kept alive he may give to us half the treasure and Sandi shall not do us harm for it. As for the woman . . ."

But when they came to look for her she had left the canoe to drift and had gone swiftly through the forest for it seems she knew their mind.

So she came in the dark to her own hut and none asked her where she had been, nor yet saw her come.

People came to her and asked her where was her husband, and when she told them that he had gone on a long journey, an old uncle, a grizzled old man, dour of heart and vengeful, was frankly sceptical.

"Sandi comes soon," he said significantly, "and there will be a great palaver, and who knows what will come of your great wealth, your goods and your ivory?"

He left her in a panic. Already her more portable treasures had vanished and she had had no redress against the brothers of Akasava, for how could she tell Sandi that she had been to these men with her great plan. And when Sandi moved in his little white ship, he had a trick of peering in most unlikely places. Suppose his devilish curiosity brought him to the Island of Fast Waters, and he found there a haltered prisoner?

She called her chief woman to her.

"Call paddlers for my fast boat. I go to Bosambo of the Ochori. He is wise, though a great lover of money."

To Bosambo she went, setting forth before the dawn light came up over the dark gum trees, and this time Bosambo did not meet her on the beach or pay her honour, but when he saw her:

"O woman," he said loftily, "I have nothing to sell! But if you have come to give me what is fair for all that you took away, I will listen to you, for my heart is soft."

She sat down before him and crossed her hands meekly. Though she was rich she was of the common people, and he was the Chief paramount and reputedly related to Sandi.

For a long time she skirted the matter which had brought her; talked of the rains and the crops, and the full river, and the strange signs that had been seen in the sky till Bosambo's stock of patience was exhausted.

"Now tell me the truth, woman, why you come here? For I am a man with many great matters to think about and the talk of women is to me like the chattering of monkeys."

And then she told him, falteringly, more or less falsely and coming to the truth unconsciously and by degrees.

Bosambo had many ears in the territory. The Ochori people go far afield, especially the fishermen, who have no respect for property in waters, and he had heard of B'laba, who beat his wife. It had been a very comforting thought to Bosambo, but now as she proceeded, his interest in B'laba was a secondary one.

". . . and these men I paid well, yet they took my treasures, my fine skins and silver, my salt and my skins, which B'laba my husband stole, and these they have hidden in a great hole in the Island of Fast Waters and they have tied B'laba by the neck to a tree and every day take food to him. Now Bosambo I will give you one sack of silver if you will find my treasures and bring them to me, but mostly if you carry away with you B'laba, my husband, for fear he speaks to Sandi."

Bosambo was a lover of money as she knew, and it was a little surprising that he did not bargain for two or even three sacks of silver.

He dismissed her graciously and as soon as night fell he took his guard of trusted men, he himself wielding a paddle for he had no room to spare in the canoe for an unnecessary paddler.

He saw the fires of the village of M'pusu as he passed, came through the gorge and into the current, and with the greatest difficulty made a landing on the island. It was a mile and a half in length, a tangle of vegetation. His journey through the bush was slow and laborious, but he had the light of a moon.

Bosambo's intentions were more or less honourable, but he had certainly no desire to encumber himself with a prisoner. His one wish was to find the treasure and to discover it without having recourse to those methods of interrogation which might lead him into trouble. As a last resort he might interview the three brothers, but this he would rather avoid . . .

There had been other visitors to the island that night.

The three brothers of the Akasava had held a council and they were uneasy men for in the first darkness of the previous night they had heard the distant rattle of a *lokali*, that signal drum which carries rumour through space. And it had said "A new spy of Sandi moves north."

One of them who had dealings with the chief of a little village made a journey to learn the news.

"Shiribi that is true," said the little chief, "for my own brother told me. There is a spy who moves in the night, a starved long man who speaks to such as he meets in the dark hours and talks of gold such as our father spoke about. Sometimes his canoe appears amongst the fishers and he asks them where treasures are hidden in the ground."

"Oh ko!" said the brother in dismay. "I think Sandi has long ears like a pig."

"Also," said the gossip, "this man takes sand from the river and pours water over it and mutters in a curious tongue. B'sambo of the Isisi saw and heard this, watching the foreigner from the beach. And they say that this man goes to all the little islands because N'dama of the Isisi has told him that in the little islands are great riches."

The man of the Akasava knew N'dama for an enemy, for his brother had once disappeared and he had gone to Sandi to find him. This was bad news indeed. He went back to his brethren and told them all that he had heard.

"If Sandi hears all that he has to hear, and if he digs in the Island of Swift Waters, there will be a rope for us," said the elder.

For there were many souvenirs of past "trading" that might be found for the digging and they had enemies who would whisper of what a spade might find.

"Let us take B'laba and the treasure and bring them to the forest, for B'laba will talk."

They went to the island at nightfall and took a stout rope from his neck, but left his hands tied. One (the youngest) was for killing him, but his wise elders overruled him. A dead man needs carrying they said. B'laba came alive to the forest behind the huts where the brothers lived, and the wives of these men heard his faint shriek and were unmoved for they had heard that sound before.

When they had finished their work they returned to the isle and with their spears uncovered the sacks of silver—the salt they had already taken to their own use.

The first sack had been lifted to the edge of the hole . . . when——

"O man I see you . . . !"

The younger of the brothers looked round with a screech of fright and reached for his spear. Before his hand closed upon it, a brother caught his arm.

He had seen the tall figure in the moonlight naked to the waist.

"Go!" he whispered and the three melted noiselessly into the bush.

Bosambo, moving cautiously through the tangle, did not so much as hear the thresh of their paddles. As he came clear of a patch of thorn bushes into a wide grove between the trees, he saw a native digging something up from the ground; evidently there was a hole there, for from time to time the man half vanished up to his waist and reappeared groaning as he flung down something heavy to the ground, something that tinkled musically in Bosambo's ears.

Here was a situation that Bosambo had not foreseen, he had hoped that the prisoner was at the other end of the island, out of sight and hearing, for he had a passionate objection to being recognized as the looter of buried silver.

Slipping off the rug he wore about his shoulders he motioned two men to follow him, and creeping silently forward as the tall figure of the digging native appeared, he leapt forward, enveloping his head in the rug, and in a few minutes the squirming prisoner was bound hand and foot.

"O man," said Bosambo softly, "if you will make a noise I will beat you! And if you fight I will kill you!"

There was need for this injunction because the prisoner was making more noise than a sensible prisoner should make and was struggling with great desperation.

"Keep the cloth over his head and carry him to the canoe," said Bosambo in a whisper.

The remainder of his paddlers shouldered the sacks and made their way back to the boat.

A healthy struggling prisoner Bosambo had not foreseen, and his canoe was level almost with the water's edge when the paddlers struck swiftly for the north.

An hour before the first light dawned in the east, Bosambo had reached the Ochori city.

"Bring this man into my hut," he commanded.

They obeyed him. It was dark in the hut. Bosambo was most desirous that he should not be seen.

"B'laba," he said softly, "I am a friend who has saved you from the woman who tied you to a tree in the little island, and from the three brothers of the Akasava, and this woman will never forgive me because I have saved you. So you must not see the face of your friend for fear you betray me. Presently I will put you in a canoe and let you drift in the waters and . . ."

He was untying the wrist of the man when his hand touched something on the prisoner's wrist and he gasped.

"O Bosambo," the voice from the bound and trussed man on the floor was hollow and breathless, "for this you shall suffer great pain!"

Bosambo did not collapse, he gripped tightly to the skin bed on which he was sitting.

"You are a fearful old bounder," roared the voice in English. "By gad! . . . I'll . . . I'll . . . !"

"Tibbetti," quavered Bosambo in coast-Arabic, "is it thou?"

He called for lights; when they came he stared down on a lank and painfully thin native, but despite his greased and blackened hair there was no difficulty in recognizing Bones. Even if he had not seen the thing on his wrist.

∙　∙　∙　∙　∙

"I was naturally fearfully annoyed," explained Bones to his interested audience at the residency, "and when he told me he had heard I was in danger and rescued me against my bally will, well that simply made me see red! The most astonishing thing, dear old Sir and Excellency, was that those bags that I thought had money in them hadn't silver at all!"

"No," said Sanders dryly.

"No," said Bones, "that is the astonishing thing about it, they were full of shells and bits of brass and flint spear-heads and things, every one of 'em. And Shiribi fellows—bad lads every one of 'em, I collected them on my way down—these ghastly fellows said that the bags were full of silver!"

"And they were not," said Sanders.

"Bits of iron, dear old Excellency," said Bones.

"Can you tell me this," Sanders was more than interested, "how long was it after you revealed yourself to Bosambo, that you examined the sacks?"

Bones screwed up his eyes which meant that he was thinking.

"About an hour."

"Tons of time for Bosambo," said Sanders and Hamilton together.

Sanders looked at his subordinate thoughtfully.

"I'm afraid you're not a master of disguise Bones—I heard about your progress from village to village. Everybody knew you but they were too polite to say so: they called you the new spy?"

"Knew me, dear old Excellency?" squeaked Bones incredulously. "But my dear old Excellency . . . Ham old lad . . . my disguise was wonderful . . . . I shan't get that beastly stain off for months. . . ."

"A perfect disguise, I agree," said Sanders, "but wandering natives do not wear wrist watches."

Bones was more interested than abashed.

"Then how the dooce do they tell the time?" he asked.

X   *THE KEEPERS OF THE TREASURE*

YEARS and years ago, *cala cala* as the saying is, when the Portuguese were in the land, came many canoes along the great river. In those days there was a river that ran through the N'gombi country—it is now an overgrown depression in the forest. Whence came this expedition nobody knew. The men camped on the edge of the Ochori country and made a fortification with the help of forced labour. Then came other men in pursuit, and there was a great battle of swords and spears, and in the end the attackers succeeded. Every defender was put to the sword, but when the victorious captain came to look for the ten great boxes which the fugitives had brought with them they were not to be found. They had been buried by somebody—legend gave credit to a score of somebodies.

From time to time adventurers had sought the hiding place; one chief of the Ochori, who was supposed to know where the boxes were hidden, had been put to the torture; commissioners had made the most careful enquiries, commanders of expeditions who were of a romantic turn of mind had dug and probed, but all to no purpose.

There remained this substance to the legend, that in a village of the Ochori three men were called The Keepers of the Treasure Place, and the office was hereditary and very old.

What treasure they guarded no man knew. They professed to have exact information, and whispered their secret to every new guardian that death appointed.

The Portuguese treasure was a common subject of gossip up and down the coast. Once Lieutenant Tibbetts had made an ineffectual search, guided by a dream. Captain Hamilton of the King's Houssas suggested a remedy for such dreams.

"Coarseness, dear old thing!" murmured Bones, shocked. "Vulgarity, dear old officer! Come, come, this will never do!"

"Did you really dream you saw the cave?" asked Sanders, interested.

"Yes, Excellency and friend. A dashed big cave in the side of the mountain. Wonderful lights, all colours, inside. And I stepped brightly into the cave an' there was a dear old johnny in a white robe, an angel or something ghastly, and he said——"

" 'Welcome, Ali Baba?' " suggested Hamilton.

Bones made a tutting noise.

The next time he went into the Ochori he came to a village reputedly built on or near the site of the treasure trove, and interviewed the chief.

"Lord, it is true that I and two very old men are keepers of this wonder which no man has seen because of the devils who sit under the trees by day and night

87

and change into a hundred leopards when man goes near them. But the place may not be told until I and the two old men die."

Bones spent a week in the forest, looking for a place where buried treasure might be, and all the time he was stalked by the slim widow who coveted the treasure. In course of time Bones went back to face the withering sarcasms of his superior officer, but the widow continued her search, for she had a rapacious lover who desired wealth—a tall, broad man who plastered his hair with clay and wore the skin of a leopard and stood around in statuesque attitudes, but did nothing much else to earn his living.

This woman, whose name was N'saki, had had three husbands and each of these died. There was nothing remarkable about their ends. They were very old, and the Dark One beckons such with great frequency. Such is the mind of man that when she offered herself to M'gama, the middle-aged chief of the village, he rejected her.

"It seems that there is a devil in you, N'saki, so that men who have loved you go quickly to the ghosts. Three Keepers of the Treasure have taken you to their huts and three have died. Now I desire to live, and all the loveliness you offer me is as nothing if I die."

N'saki was a rich woman, her three husbands having been plentifully blessed. Also she was beautiful to look upon and so clever that she read men's minds. She was eighteen, slim as a reed, and childless. And she greatly wished to be the wife of the chief of the village, who reputedly shared the secret of the buried treasure. Some said this was dead ivory and some that it was white man's wealth. Her handsome lover favoured the latter theory.

"All you have done is for nothing, woman," he said irritably. "Three dying men have you had in your hands and none told you the Magic Ground, and their places have been filled."

"O N'kema-M'libi!" she pleaded. "I did what was to be done; some I choked a little, so that they were frightened, but because of their ju-ju they feared worse to tell me. Now M'gama is a greater coward, and if he would have had me as his wife I would have made him speak. I will ask him again, and if he will not take me I will go to Bosambo and tell him of this treasure, for I think that M'gama knows of the little yellow cup."

Now this was true, that there had appeared in M'gama's hut a yellow cup of beautiful design, and wise men knew it was gold, but none was so wise that he could guess where M'gama had found it. N'saki guessed.

"I will find a way," she said.

Eventually she found it, with the aid of a man from Senegal and another from the Kroo coast, who were at that moment newly arrived on the coast from the city and state of New York.

One of these was from Dakar, and his name was Fendi. He was a black man, Nubian black as distinct from the brown men of the river. The French did not like Fendi, who spoke three languages well, and since the French are masters of Senegal their antipathy counted. They did not like his influence or the prosperity which enabled him to live in enviable luxury, but their first objection to him was his poisonous contact with civilization. For Fendi had been to France, had fought in the ring both in Paris and in New York, and had been expelled from the latter city at the instance of the emigration authorities ("Where'n hell's this Dakar, anyway?" asked the puzzled official.)

Fendi had joined up with certain tough forces in Harlem, where he had lived for five years, and his American adventures had terminated with a gang fight in which razors, automatics and broken glass had figured conspicuously.

They took Fendi out of the hospital whither unloving hands had borne him and put him on a boat bound for the coast.

"Come back and we'll bump you," said an official significantly.

"I shouldn't be the first gen'leman you've bumped," said Fendi defiantly.

He took away with him from the United States enough money to live (by Dakar standards) in comfort for the rest of his life.

With him was exported one Mr. Seluki, a native of Liberia and a Master of Arts of the University of Romeville (Oklahoma). That M.A. set him back two hundred bucks. Seluki stopped off at Dakar, and, with his friend, went up to St. Louis, which lies at the end of the railway. St. Louis was dull; Dakar was slow. They came back to the capital and settled down with certain undesirable elements in the lower town.

Fendi's pride in his home town brought no enthusiastic response from his companion.

"Yuh! That Governor General's palace is fine, but gimme Little Old!"

In this familiar way did he refer to the Empire City of New York.

In the lodging house where they stayed they met a Christian, American-trained native who had worked with the missionaries until he was found out. He had stories to tell of a land flowing with milk and honey—a raw, rich country stiff with dead ivory. "Why, fellers, there was a guy from Liberia, a nigger named Bosambo, who went in and cleaned up, and he's worth a million dollars if he's worth talking about. And have you heard about the buried treasure? A million dollars' worth, and any guy could snitch it."

Fendi listened and was fascinated; Seluki had heard of Bosambo and the treasure before.

A month later the two boarded an Elder Dempster boat southward-bound.

"What you gotta do," counselled the Christian man, "is to play native. You go in fresh an' start cracking English and this guy Sanders'll fire you out so that you'll never feel the grass rustle under your feet. And don't pull any missionary stuff neither. He won't stand for Allelulia niggers. Get him right and he's dead easy."

To the residency on a certain afternoon came two humble natives and Seluki, who talked Bomongo fluently, was the spokesman.

"Lord, we wish to go to our cousin Bosambo," he said glibly.

Mr. Commissioner Sanders surveyed the men coldly.

"You are Liberian, but this man is from Senegal," he said.

Fendi was startled This was the first white man he had ever met who could differentiate one tribe from another at a glance.

"Also you must tell me why you wish to go to the Ochori. Once before a poor relation of Bosambo came here and there was trouble, for Bosambo is no rich man with alms to give."

"Nor are we poor men, lord," said Seluki eagerly. "I bring a bag of silver and I have a book for money."

He produced before the sceptical Commissioner a bag of veritable cash. The three boxes that had been landed on the beach were not opened.

"Go with God," said Sanders, "you and the Senegalese. But this is a wild country, and here there are many bad men. You shall not blame me if your money goes in the night."

Fendi smiled to himself.

They engaged paddlers from Chubiri to take them up stream, but long before they reached the Ochori country Bosambo had news of their coming, for Sanders had sent him a pigeon message, but, as the Commissioner had not mentioned the bag of silver, Bosambo's greeting lacked cordiality.

The long journey up river had been profitable in one respect. Fendi, like other natives of the coast, had a smattering of all the dialects; by the time they reached the Ochori city he was as proficient in Bomongo as his companions. He was not particularly happy.

"This country is one large morgue," he grumbled. "There isn't ten cents in any of these villages. Compared with them, a Harlem slum's like Riverside Drive. You've certainly got me for a sucker."

"You haven't seen the big stuff yet," said Seluki mysteriously, and Fendi grunted.

Fendi had the instincts of a gangster, and, providing there were any pickings to pick, he saw the immense possibility of this land which had distance without communication.

"It seems to me," he said, the day before they reached the Ochori, "there's no gat in the country, except them that the soldiers have got down to the mouth of the river."

Seluki explained the law. Firearms were prohibited. He had already told his friend that.

"I know," said Fendi, "but naturally I thought there would be a bit of graft here; someone must be running guns on the side."

He was impressed by the bulk of Bosambo, a little irritated by his hauteur.

"I see you, man," said Bosambo, addressing his fellow countryman Seluki. "I see you, yet I do not know you. I have nothing to give you, and when you have slept you shall take your paddlers and return to your own home. Who am I that I should keep hungry men from Liberia?"

"O Bosambo," said Seluki loftily, "I ask nothing of you. I come as a giver."

He clapped his hands, and one of his men lugged forward the bag of silver, and Seluki carefully unrolled the top. Bosambo looked and blinked.

"Ah, now I see that you are my friend," he said enthusiastically. "Tell me, brother, does Sandi know you brought this great treasure for me?"

Seluki swallowed something.

"Sandi knows I have the money," he said, "but no man knows that I have brought this to you; for this is my own. Yet I will let you take all that your two hands can hold."

Bosambo stepped down from his stool and was about to plunge his hands into the bag, then stopped.

"First I will pray in my hut, for I am of the true faith, Seluki, and I will ask the guidance of the Prophet."

He was gone some time. When he reappeared he walked quickly to the bag, thrust in his hands and arms to his elbows, and Fendi gasped as he saw the amount that was removed. For some curious reason money was not only held in his hands, but covered his arms like huge silver spangles.

"O ko!" said Seluki, in dismay.

Bosambo went straight to his hut, deposited the silver, and washed off the thick copal gum which he had spread on his arms. When he came back he was in the most amiable frame of mind.

"You shall sleep in my best hut, and to-night I will have a great dance for you. To-morrow you shall sit in my palaver house on my right hand and my left, and the people shall do homage to you. As for that bag of silver, I will put it in a safe place."

"I know nothing safer than my own hut, Bosambo," said his guest with some acerbity.

There was a dance that night which was witnessed by two other strangers to the city. N'saki had come a long journey to make a palaver with Bosambo about a certain gold cup of curious design.

After the dance Fendi saw a comely girl edging towards the select crescent of spectators. With a vanity which is eternal in man he thought her eyes were for him, and, detaching himself from the guests at a moment when all eyes were for the swaying bodies of the dancers, he came up to her.

"O woman, I am the man you seek."

Here he was wrong; but N'saki was an opportunist and knew him, by the quick reputation he had acquired, to be both rich and powerful.

"To-night I shall sit in the little hut which has been made for me," he said. "Let us talk together and I will tell you of people like none other in the world."

She shook her head, which means "yes," and that night she went to him, and, when she had the opportunity of talking, she told him of M'gama and the little golden cup . . .

Three days after, he took from one of his boxes a bundle of cloth and un-rolling this exposed four automatics with appropriate etceteras. He and Seluki left, ostensibly on a hunting trip, accompanied by three bearers. Near to the village of M'gama the bearers were to be sent back, but before that could happen an unfortunate thing occurred. One of the bearers was a spy of Bosambo's, sent to report on the doings of the strangers. He was an inquisitive man and he was curious to know what were the contents of the little bags which the adventurers carried strapped to their shoulders.

In the dark of the night he opened one and saw the automatic and the spare magazines and took counsel with his fellows.

"O ko! These men carry the little-little guns that say 'ha ha', and this Bosambo must know."

As they squatted over their fire Fendi rolled over to his companion and woke him.

"These niggers have lamped the gats, Selu'. They gotta be bumped."

The "bumping" occurred at daybreak. Two of the bearers fell in their tracks and never knew what hit them. The third, the spy, ran for it, the bullets whistling after him. It was Seluki who dropped him at the edge of the small stream Busini, and Fendi, running up, saw the water pink with blood and the swirl of a quickly moving crocodile.

He went back, and with his companion hid the bodies of the carriers he had slain.

"If that 'jane' plays square we'll be outa this country before there's a breeze. French territory's forty-five miles due north—and I'm a French subject!"

The "jane" was waiting an hour's march away from the scene of the tragedy, and with her her tall and statuesque lover, who leaned on a spear and said nothing.

Her first words were disconcerting.

"Show me your little-little gun that killed Bosambo's men."

Being vain, Fendi showed her the automatic. To his surprise she handled the weapon scientifically.

"These I have seen," she said. "Once there was a soldier of Sandi who loved me for a week and he showed me these mysteries."

She pulled back the safety catch, deftly removed the magazine and replaced it, before she handed it back to the impatient gangster.

Her plan was simple. On the rind of the moon M'gama and the two old keepers of the treasure went out into the forest, throwing curses behind them and leaving their ju-jus to guard their path. So that any who followed or spied on them would be stricken blind and presently would be devoured inch by inch by a most terrible lizard.

"He will come this night," she said. "We will rest here until the trees go to sleep on the ground, and then I will show you the way."

At sunset, when the shadows of the trees ran for enormous distances, she walked ahead of them into a gloom that became instantly night. The rind of the moon was in the sky when they reached their destination, and they squatted within sight of the forest path down which presently would come M'gama and the two trustees.

Punctually to the minute three figures came out of the gloom and vanished, with M'saki and the two strangers on their trail. For an hour they walked noiselessly until they came to a small knoll where stood four trees, and at the foot of the knoll M'gama and his two companions halted and performed mysterious rites, and would have gone away again, only Fendi and his companions stood in their path.

92

"Now," said Fendi, when the three old men were tied securely, "tell me where this beautiful treasure is hidden."

He questioned them all night, using various methods. One old man died in the process, but the other two were dumb. He had a brief consultation with Seluki.

"We'll have to let up on these two old guys," he said. "Give 'um a rest, and maybe to-night they'll squeal."

"What about the 'jane'?" asked Seluki.

Fendi looked over his shoulder at the girl and her motionless lover.

"They've *gotta* be bumped," he said.

It was not two days or three days or yet four when the last of the living men spoke, and for six hours Fendi and his friend dug into the solid earth. They recovered many things that remained of the loot of a forgotten African monastery, filched by Portuguese filibusters; cups and chalices and golden vessels, and a rotting bag of gold coins.

The lover did not assist in the digging, but he helped to carry the treasure to the river that trickled into the French territory, and which was eight miles distant. He even stirred himself to steal a big canoe from an upriver village. He chose up river because the canoe floated down with a very small expenditure of energy. In the canoe the treasure was loaded.

"All is well now," said N'saki, "and I will tell you an island where you may go and hide."

"Sure!" said Fendi. "But let's go back and see if there's anything we've left behind."

The four trudged back to the treasure hole.

"O man," said Fendi, feeling stealthily for his gun, "look deep in that hole and see if there is anything we have forgotten."

The lover staggered forward and bent over, and Fendi's gun jerked up and spat fire. He turned, his pistol poised, but the girl had vanished. He saw an agitated movement of long grass and fired twice, but when he dashed in the direction she had taken she had gone, and he could not find her.

"That's bad. We've got to catch that dame before she gets to the river," he said.

And then, unrolling his pack, he made a discovery.

"Where's that other gun?" he asked, and his face went grey.

For N'saki had once a lover who taught her the mysteries of automatics.

Again he blundered through some undergrowth where he had detected a movement, and Seluki was close on his heels.

"I see you," said a hard little voice.

The men were so close to her that she could not miss . . .

A pigeon came to headquarters. Bones was hustled in the middle of the night on to the *Zaire* with twenty soldiers, and, steaming night and day, stopping only at the woodings, he came to the Ochori village, and a very serious Bosambo was waiting.

"Lord, there are guns in this country," he said. "Two men you sent to me went out in search of treasure, and they shot my private man. And because Sandi has said we must not go against guns, I sent for you."

Two of his fighting regiments were ready for the march. He strode by the side of Bones through the Ochori forest, and presently came to the village of M'gama —but M'gama was not there. Trackers found his body and brought Lieutenant Tibbetts to the spot. Earth had been turned here, and Bones pointed.

"Set your young men to dig with their spears."

They dug for a short time and presently they found Fendi and his friend, but nothing else.

"These men have been shot," said Bosambo. "Here are the little guns."

Four pistols lay in the hole. M'saki had no further use for them; she was paddling a laden canoe towards the French territory, singing a song that was all about her dead lover and the treasure that would bring her many successors.

D'MINI, the dancing girl, was a great giver. She gave all that clever feet could give to the old king who lives beyond the Ghost Mountains and at night, when he sat nodding before the big fire which burnt in front of his fine hut—and when it was death to his captains and servants, and even to his wives if they dared so much as to sneeze, and worse than death to a dancing woman if he came awake and found her motionless—she would dance and never stop through his slumberings, until her breath came in thin, whistling gasps and her wet and palpitating body was one great ache and weariness.

She gave to M'suru, the old king's captain, who was slightly mad; and he took all she had to give and showed her his broad hunting sword with its keen edge, and told her what would happen to her if she spoke of their friendship; and she gave presents of skin and ivory that came her way at odd intervals to an old woman who looked after her, and whom she believed was her mother. And in return the old woman gave her dreams.

Stretched on the skin bed, D'mini listened with closed eyes.

". . . Long, long ago, *cala cala*, the White King came across the Ghost Mountains, and with him a tall chief who had a shining eye, and him they called Tibbetti. And even the old king was afraid . . . In this land beyond the mountains, all is kindness; and the White King, whose name is Sandi, will let no woman be flogged and no man be chopped in the night . . . and the man with the shining eye is his son, and he is very beautiful—as far as white people can be beautiful—and very kind to women. . . ."

With these dreams D'mini, the dancing girl, eased the hard way of her life, so that when the old man, in a fit of wrath, had her whipped for some fault (M'suru knew why she danced so lifelessly) she fixed her mind and her soul on the son of Sandi, who was kind to women.

Then one day her own brother, who lived in a distant village, spoke against the old king, and was taken by the king's soldiers and put to torture . . .

And neither that night nor the next did M'suru speak to her, and when she went to dance before the old man in the light of the fire, his counsellors drove her away; and she knew that her end was near.

In the dark of the night she took a canoe, and paddled down the swift stream. Near to the gorge, where the waters run with such force that no paddler dare go farther, she came to land, and went on foot towards the high hills which in the cold months are powdered with white dust. Beyond these lay a land ruled by a King whose son was tall, and was kind to women. . . .

•   •   •   •   •

"The first of next month, dear old officer," said Bones, with an air of unconcern, "is my birthday."

"Let us keep to the more important matter of pants," said Captain Hamilton, coldly.

They sat in the sweltering clothes store; ranged on long benches were piles of garments designed for issue. There were shirts—khaki, and shorts—drill, boots —tropical, puttees—service; all the sartorial paraphernalia of the strenuous military life.

Bones sighed heavily.

"Why not, dear old Ham, send back to G.H.Q. and say you found 'em?" he suggested, hopefully. "After all, dear old Ham, if we say we've got sixty-nine pairs of pants and that perfectly ghastly quartermaster says that we've only got forty-nine, ought there not, as it were, dear old officer, to be rejoicing at headquarters? Now if I was at headquarters, and I found that somebody had got twenty-nine pants more than they ought to have, I'd send a wire saying 'Get on with the good work, old thing——' "

"But, you poor, addle-pated greyhound, we haven't got any surplus pants at all. We've got just the number we should have. The return you made was as wrong as——"

Hamilton was weary and impatient.

"In that case," demanded the exasperated Bones, "what's all the bother about, dear old thing? Simply send the old josser a note saying 'Dear Sir: Re yours of even date, pants found, all is well. Love to auntie, kiss baby, Bill'."

Hamilton sat down in a hard chair and mopped his streaming forehead.

"Do you mind going away and drowning yourself?" he asked—gently, for him.

"O Abiboo"—Captain Hamilton called the sergeant of Houssas waiting outside the hut—"bring all the books to my room."

Bones had a brilliant inspiration.

"Listen, Ham," he said, eagerly, "I've got it! All these pants are in pairs, dear old thing. Do you think the naughty old quartermaster is reckoning two to a pair? How's that?"

"Get out!"

It was in the very dark hours of a sweltering morning that, poring over Bones' illegible returns he found the error. Bones in some mysterious fashion had added the sizes of military pants to the quantities.

Though the next day was not Bones' birthday, he came to breakfast to find a stale gingerbread cake which had been sent some six months before by a misguided relative, and on it were seven large tallow candles, all burning offensively at various angles.

"I'm taking time by the forelock," said Hamilton. "The candles are not for your years, but for your mentality."

Bones, with great dignity, lifted the cake, carried it to the door and kicked it into the parade ground.

He was very silent that day, and in the evening, as they sat in the cool of the verandah, drinking coffee that refused to get cool, he revealed his startling resolve.

"I'm going to turn over a new leaf, dear old Ham. My youth is passed, dear old boy. I am a man, Ham. As Shakespeare so dinkily puts it, life's a dashed serious thing. No more giddy frivolity, dear old captain. Do you agree with me, Excellency?"

"Quite," said Mr. Commissioner Sanders, who was thinking of something else.

"I'm going to burn the banjulele and take a course in bookkeeping. There's a fellow advertising in one of those magazines who teaches the whole beastly business in thirteen lessons."

"An unlucky number for you," said Hamilton.

"Nothing but duty from now on, old friend," said Bones, firmly. "I've got the thing completely settled in my mind: 7 to 8, Swedish exercises, dear old boy; 8 to 9, study of military law; 9 to 11, bookkeeping; 11 to 1, military duties as per schedule; one hour for lunch, or perhaps a little less; 2 to 4, strategy and tactics; 4 to 4.30, a simple cup of tea, dear old boy, and maybe a thin slice of bread and butter; 4.30 to 7, a little biology, or maybe zoology; bed at 8."

"If you would spend a couple of hours a day learning to write so that intelligent people could read your infernal——"

"Catagraphy?" suggested Bones, helpfully. "That means getting up two hours earlier, but I'll do it, Ham—for your sake, sweetheart." He dodged the book that Hamilton hurled at him.

For two days Bones kept to some kind of programme. He was certainly invisible between 2 in the afternoon and 5. He was also invisible most of the other hours of the day when Hamilton wanted him. But, curiously enough, he remained very serious, and when Hamilton found him voluntarily instructing a squad in the art of bayonet fighting, it did seem that the new leaf was well and truly turned. But, as Hamilton said, Bones lived a lifetime every three days, and you never quite knew what the next day would bring.

Bones smiled archly when he heard this.

"What will my birthday bring, dear old Ham? I saw a little parcel that came from H.Q. yesterday——"

"That was a bottle of tasteless castor oil," said Hamilton, coldly. "You may have a half, but I never intended it as a present."

Sanders chuckled.

"If you had given me good notice, Bones, I'd have got something from London—a box of chocolates——"

"Or a box of bricks—or better still, a ready reckoner."

But Bones was not perturbed.

"I've got a ready reckoner, old Ham, but I want another—mine is last year's. Now, if anybody wants to buy me a present I'll tell you what I'd like. Braces, dear old Ham, or a pair of jolly little links—crystal and diamonds——"

Even as Bones was speaking, a present was on its way.

M'suru-b'langa, the warrior of the old king who lives beyond the Ghost Mountains, came down into the Ochori country with twenty huntsmen, for they were on the trail of the woman D'mini, and in any case were contemptuous of boundaries. And so trespassing in forbidden lands, they came upon another hunting party under Bosambo, paramount chief of the Ochori, by courtesy called "king."

The parties met in the forest, and Bosambo, a stickler for the law when it was on his side, stared at the strange men.

"O, Bosambo, I see you," said M'suru, with the cool familiarity of an equal. "Have you and your young men seen a woman pass this way?"

"Whose dog are you?" asked Bosambo, politely.

M'suru stiffened.

"I am M'suru who stands next to the great king," he said.

Bosambo could be heavily sarcastic. He was all that now.

"O ko! And now you stand next to the king of the Ochori, M'suru, and only my guard speak to me with spears in their hands."

M'suru hesitated. Here was a famous breaker of necks, if stories were true; one without fear or thought of kings or ghosts or devils. A broad, immense man without fat.

He dropped his killing spears at his feet, and his men followed his example.

"Now you shall tell me, M'suru, why you are in my fine land with spears, so that I may make a book for Sandi my master. Sit."

M'suru squatted on the ground, trembling with rage, for only the king in his own land could say "sit" or "stand," and he was a proud man.

"This woman D'mini has spoken against the king because he gave her brother to the skins. Also she is a witch. For when she dances, all men must dance. Therefore, I come to take her back to the master so that she may die."

Bosambo looked at the speaker for a long time before he spoke.

"If you kill all women who make men dance, then the world will die, for there will be no woman left alive," he said, dryly. "Go back to your land, M'suru, for this is the land of my king, who does not kill women nor sew men into sacks. This palaver is finished."

M'suru rose and gathered up his spears.

"This I will do, Bosambo."

His voice was almost humble, his manner was surprisingly deferential. Bosambo, who was not impressed by sudden humility, lifted his shield to the level of his chin.

The man turned in his tracks, and, in accordance with custom, Bosambo turned too, for the immemorial law is that enemies, or potential enemies, who are parting in friendship, turn back to back.

"Watch!"

The voice, thin and shrill with fear, came from a reedy patch of coarse grass. He turned swiftly, saw the spear leave M'suru's hand, and caught it on the boss of his shield. Then, as the stranger turned to fly, Bosambo's shoulder went backward and forward. . . . The spear caught M'suru between spine and armpit, and he died instantly.

"Follow," said Bosambo to his men, as M'suru's hunters vanished.

Then he went back to the reeds.

"Come to me, woman," he said, and the grass shook and heaved, and into his sight came D'mini, the woman.

She was very slim and gracefully made, as he could see, for she wore neither cloth nor girdle. She had the thin nose of the Arab people, and her hair was straight and long. She looked at him with big eyes, and did not seem afraid.

"I am D'mini, of the Great People," she said; "and I seek the tall son of your King, who is kind to women; him they call Tibbetti."

Bosambo stared at her in astonishment.

"O woman, he is not for you; but I will send a book of your words to Sandi, so that he shall know what to do for you. Afterwards I will send you in a canoe to him for judgment."

When his men returned from their chase with only one bloody spear to show, he went back to the Ochori village he had left that morning, and sent a swift runner to the Ochori city, carrying a tiny cigarette-paper on which he had scrawled his tidings. And the pigeon who carried this came perilously to headquarters with a hawk on his tail.

Sanders was dozing in a chair when the news arrived. Pigeons were frequent visitors—not often did they bring news of high political doings, but this once the message that the little messenger brought was sufficient to set the bugles blowing, for Sanders knew the methods of the old king who lived beyond the Ghost Mountains.

He had no blame for Bosambo. The customs of the land were well defined. He did not doubt that the Ochori chief had struck in self-defence—but the old king was a foreigner, and war with him meant complications in half-a-dozen European capitals. And war was inevitable, for this man who had been old since the beginning of the world (according to the river legend) was the head and commander of a highly organized fighting force.

"Condemn all women who make wars!" he said, cold-bloodedly. "Send word to Bosambo to meet Bones at the joining of the rivers, and to bring the woman with him."

"How much trouble is there going to be?" asked Captain Hamilton of the Houssas.

"Five thousand rounds of small arm and two hundred shrapnel," said Sanders, practically. "Let us be on the safe side. Bones can go first on the *Wiggle*. We will follow him as a reserve. If we make too big a show we shall flatter the old devil."

Bones was indulging in his afternoon studies, oblivious to bugles and war, for he had eaten Yorkshire pudding for lunch, and in the coldest of climates Yorkshire pudding is a deadly soporific.

Hamilton found him lying uncovered on his bed, a mosquito gauze over his bare feet. His purple pyjamas were striped with pale lemon zigzags—Hamilton clutched the doorpost for support.

"Arise, and gird your lions—Venus," he snarled.

Bones blinked himself awake.

"All correct, sir," he said, hoarsely, as he brought his large feet to the floor. "Thinking, old boy—not asleep, just thinking, old Excellency. What's the morning like?"

"Very much like the afternoon," said Hamilton. "The chief wants you."

The dazed Bones groped for his mosquito boots.

"And by gosh, he shall have me, old sir," he said, firmly. "As jolly old Browning says—we've only got to die once. Personally speakin' that never cheered me up. If you died more than once you'd get used to it, old Ham. Do you see my meanin'? That's philosophy."

He changed his mind about his boots, grabbed an armful of flimsy wear and vanished behind a curtain. Hamilton heard the splash of water and sundry gasps. A few minutes later Bones, lightly attired in his underwear, appeared.

"Horrible," said Hamilton. "Your mother should have done something about those knees of yours."

Against Sanders and his administration the old king's heart was very sour. There had already been two encounters, one which might have ended in the destruction of the old man's deadly regime but for the interest which European Powers had in this No Man's Land which was claimed by every man. He had grown in strength and in arrogance, so that once when Sanders had asked for a palaver to deal with certain outstanding matters, he could afford to reply tardily and with insolence.

When the news came to him of M'suru's death he lost little time. Within forty-eight hours his war-drums had summoned two fighting regiments and they were on their way to the pass, the one practicable track which crosses the Ghost Mountains.

His task was not a simple one. The Northern Ochori were normally antagonistic to their chief, and friendly to the old king. There was a certain amount of intercourse and trading between the two tribes, and they must not be antagonized, since an unfriendly nation, however weak, holding one end of the pass, would be an everlasting danger to the arrogant old man. So that a march through the Ochori country was impossible because there was no line of demarcation between the friendly and the unfriendly section of the population. His regiments could march laterally along the western foot-hills and the mountains until they came to the river. This they did, their canoes being floated down to them through that impossible channel whose current was so strong that no canoe had ever passed up what was literally a watery slope.

The first regiment had not crossed the pass before Bosambo heard. His rendezvous with Bones was three hours' journey by river, and he was waiting at the junction of the streams when the little *Wiggle* came painfully round the bluff.

"Lord, there is trouble here," said the chief, "and all because of this woman, who is, as I think, no better than she should be."

He had brought the girl aboard, and she stood aloof from the suspicious guards that surrounded her, a dainty figure of a girl, watching the tall young man interestedly. For the moment, Bones gave her little attention. Most wars began this way, and the woman in the case was as a rule most uninteresting.

When Bones sat down to an examination on tactics and strategy under the disapproving eyes of his superior his papers were usually marked well under the figure at which a studious young officer can pass. But Bones in theory and Bones in practice were two entirely different individuals. He gave his instructions briefly, and Bosambo, well acquainted with the Tibbetti of action, listened and noted. So many men were to go across the river to hold that point where the stream narrows; so many old canoes were to be chained prow to stern across the river itself; this Ochori regiment with a machine-gun detachment of Houssas was to occupy the rising ground at the only place where the old king's forces could land.

Now the man who commanded the forces was the Chief Mofolobo, the old king's hunter, a very cunning man who had in mind his master's last instructions.

"Eat up the Ochori and bring back the woman D'mini before Sandi and his soldiers come. But if there are soldiers of Sandi you shall not fight them, but by cunning steal the woman and secretly slay the leader of the white men, so that the hearts of the soldiers shall be like wind on the waters of the river. Do this and let no man know that the king of the Great People struck."

When Mofolobo's scouts came at night to the chained canoes, and they took back word to him, he knew that the white man and his soldiers had arrived. He drew back his canoes and sent only one to make a portage beyond the barrier of boats, and that canoe was filled with terrible men. . . .

Bones had time to see the cause of the threatened war that night—she had not ceased to look at him when he was in sight. And now she sat before him, rapt, hypnotized by his splendour.

"O D'mini," he said, "there will be a great war because of you, and I think many men will die."

She nodded her dissent.

"Lord, that will not be, for often I have heard the old king say that he would not send his regiments against Sandi your King because of all the trouble that came to him *cala cala*. Also, lord, I know the heart of M'suru." She shivered. "He stood next to the king."

Bones was looking at her interestedly. He had seen her type before—a throwback to an old Arab ancestry.

"What will I do with you, D'mini?" he asked. "For you are not of any people."

She was breathing quickly, her great brown eyes fixed on his.

"Lord, let me be your servant, and I will work for you and tend your garden. . . ."

Bones shook his head with a fearful grin which she thought was very beautiful.

"Of that we shall speak to-morrow," he said, and replied to her other offer with greater emphasis.

Before the sun set he went to inspect his sentries, and found that Bosambo had anticipated him.

"Master," said the chief, "it has come to me that the old king will not fight you because you are white, but he will try to carry by cunning what he cannot do by battle. Bring your ship nearer to the bank, where my soldiers are sleeping, and no harm shall come to you."

But here Bones returned a definite negative. Bosambo's troops were encamped at a place where the current had scooped out the shore into a little bay, and he had no desire to be caught at any point where he had not a field of fire in three directions. He brought the *Wiggle* to one of the promontories, moored her with long hawsers, and before he went to bed that night set his guards at certain vital points.

"Where is the woman D'mini?" he asked Abiboo, never dreaming that she was not ashore.

"Lord, she sits by your door and will not move."

And there Bones found her; nor could she be persuaded either to go ashore or to find another sleeping place. He would have insisted, but she gave him a perfectly natural reason why she should remain close to one in authority, and he went into his cabin and had no sooner closed the door when he felt the pressure of her resting back against it.

"Deuced awkward!" said Bones.

He laid his two automatics on a small table by the side of his bed, stretched himself on the mattress and in a few minutes was asleep. No noise disturbed him, and the lightest sound would have brought him awake. Not even the posted sentries heard or saw the canoe that came upstream in the shadow of the bank.

"The woman I cannot get," said Mofolobo to his confidant, "but the young man with the shining eye sleeps in the middle of his big canoe."

Bones slept on peacefully. There must have been some slight sound, because he began to dream. It was his birthday . . . he was dimly conscious of the fact, even in his sleep. And there was a great party at headquarters, and everybody brought presents—all sorts of improbable people . . . the old vicar he knew in Guildford, and his housemaster, and that ghastly drill instructor at Sandhurst. They were all seated round the table, and before each was a priceless gift . . . . diamonds. . . .

"I don't care for diamonds, dear old thing," murmured Bones, and sat up.

He had heard nothing consciously, but the undermind of him had made a deep record, and he was instantly awake.

He moved stealthily to the door, pistol in hand. He heard a shot, and another, and the swift "swish" of paddles.

"Tried to bring me a birthday present!" said Bones, and flung open the door.

Something fell against his leg and pushed him back. He switched on the light, and looked down into the dead eyes of D'mini, the dancer, who had given him life.

ONCE UPON a time a Secretary of State for the Colonies (as he was then styled) invented a new office, and filled it instantly with a relative of his. This new official was styled Inspector of Native Territories and Protectorates. Later the rank was changed to Inspector-General, but the salary remained the same, £1,500 a year and generous allowances.

There had been successive Inspector-Generals, energetic ones, easy-going ones who spent most of their time on leave, but there had never been a really nasty Inspector-General till Major Commander Banks was appointed. He was a terribly hasty man, who stood six foot three in his stockings, a broad-shouldered, fair-haired, handsome, god-like creature, if one could imagine a god that had run slightly to fat.

Nobody knew very much about him except that he was well off, had been an officer in the army, and that he had married four times. The heavy mortality among his wives was understood by those who had the misfortune to be brought into touch with him. He was a carping bully. His attitude at best was one of conscious condescension. He seemed to find a delight in bringing misery to all who for their sins came under his dominion.

He broke two Commissioners and an Inspector of Police in the first year of his service. He drove into retirement the best administrator the territories had ever had. He so tortured an aged and inefficient paymaster over his accounts that one morning he was found dead with a revolver by his side. His manners were poisonous; he was hated through fifteen degrees of latitude; and when news came to Sanders that, for the first time in his three years' tour of office, Major Commeder Banks was paying a visit to the River, the faces of his two subordinates fell, for the Inspector-General had a military as well as a civil jurisdiction.

"To-night we start on those company and store accounts, Bones," said Hamilton, seriously. "I'll help you, and the Commissioner will lend you his clerk."

"Leave it to Bones," said Lieutenant Tibbetts, but half-heartedly. "This naughty old Banks won't rattle me, dear old Ham."

"He won't rattle you, he'll murder you," said Hamilton shortly.

Through the hot night he and Bones pored over a smudged and often corrected ledger.

"What's this two pounds four and six?" asked Hamilton.

"Two pounds four and six," said Bones, promptly.

Hamilton groaned. Again his quick pen went up and down the column, and again the total was wrong.

"Perhaps it's twenty-four and six?" suggested Bones, helpfully.

It was. Hamilton made the correction . . . five minutes later found another error. The ledger was a sad sight when they had finished with it.

"The only thing to do is to start a fresh book, get a couple of clerks working day and night, and by the time his nibs arrives we'll have everything shipshape."

But his nibs came a day too soon. Commeder Banks was, curiously enough, a man who elected to live on the Coast, a very rich man. He had a small steam yacht which had been worked out to the Coast, and it was his joy to pounce on a Tuesday upon a shivering community that had not expected him until Friday.

He came blustering up to the residency, and with him a slim, pale, frightened girl.

"You're Hamilton, eh?" he boomed, and shook the offered hand limply. "And you're Tibbetts?"

"Glad to meet you, dear old Inspector," said Bones, "and your charming daughter, dear old sir——"

Banks' face went as black as thunder.

"My wife," he snapped. "And what do you mean, sir, by calling me 'dear old Inspector?' Discipline is slack here, Sanders, very slack."

" 'Mr. Sanders,' " said Sanders quietly.

For a second their eyes met, the steel and the faded blue, and for once in his life Major Banks was uncomfortable.

"Emmie, you know these people?" he said to the nervous girl. "Mr. Sanders, Tibbetts, Hamilton." He introduced them with a sweep of his hand and walked in front of Sanders into the residency.

Lunch was a trial for everybody except Major Banks. He talked incessantly to everybody except Bones. Evidently that young man had offended him beyond hope of pardon, and it made matters no easier that Bones devoted his marked attention to Mrs. Banks. But that was because Bones' attentions were invariably well marked.

She was very pretty in a scared way. Sanders judged her to be in the region of twenty-four—she was, in fact, two years younger, and had married her present husband when she was seventeen.

"What you ought to see, dear old Mrs. Banks, is the N'gombi territory——"

"Don't call my wife 'dear old Mrs. Banks!' " bellowed the Major, red in the face; and then he glared at his wife. "The key, my dear!"

He fumbled in his pocket, produced a small Yale key, and Sanders saw the girl shrink back as though she had been struck. The Inspector-General roared with laughter.

"I'll bet you don't know what that means, my dear fellow? Do you think I lock her up when she's naughty? Not a bit of it. She knows—ask her!"

There was a most tense and uncomfortable moment. Sanders moved uneasily in his chair. The big man waved his finger playfully at his wife.

"No flirtations, Emmie darling! No more Freddies!"

"I never gave him the key, James," she quavered. "You know it's not true."

He silenced her with a gesture. That was all the reference that was made to the mysterious key and the incident in the past which he held over her head like a whip. But it was characteristic of him that, whatever the key signified, he carried it with him day and night, and would produce it before strangers to humiliate her.

He spent the afternoon examining reports in Sanders' office. They were mainly written in Sanders' own neat hand, and he read them through word by word, checking certain tables showing taxation with a little book that he had brought with him.

"What is this, Sanders?" he said, suddenly. "This doesn't seem right. The N'gombi paid twenty-eight thousand kilos of rubber—you show thirteen."

"That is the Lower N'gombi," said Sanders coldly. "You will find the Upper N'gombi produced fifteen."

The Major shook his head.

"Not very much for a big territory, you know, Mr. Sanders," he said disparagingly. "You ought to get twice as much."

"That is a matter for you to discuss with the Government," said Sanders, in his iciest tone. "I am only authorized to collect twenty-eight thousand. I will note your strictures and report them to Whitehall."

"I'm passing no strictures," said the Major, hastily.

He had been warned against Sanders; knew that the Commissioner had many influential friends at home. He made no further comment, but it was not difficult to see that he had passed on some of the dislike he felt for Bones to the Commissioner.

At dinner that night he was insufferable. He bullied his wife, contradicted Sanders, silenced Hamilton, and would have done the same to Bones, but Bones was a very difficult man to suppress.

"These territories should be reorganized. They're run in the most haphazard fashion——"

"Not at all, dear old Inspector," said Bones blandly. "That's where you're wrong, that's where you're quite wrong, my dear old sir."

The Major glared at him. Bones was unabashed.

"Is it usual for a subaltern officer to give the lie—I repeat, give the lie—to a high official of state?" he asked.

"Quite wrong, dear old Inspector, and I'm glad you know it! I couldn't help thinking, when you were contradicting dear old Excellency just now, what perfectly ghastly bad form it was."

The Major spluttered and was silent. Hamilton quaked for his subaltern. He quaked a little more when Bones told a story to the girl who was sitting by his side—a story that brought a smile to her pale face.

"Emmie, my dear." The Inspector-General's voice was silky, but in his hand he held the key. "Don't forget, my dear."

He turned his head by accident at that moment, and caught Sanders' eye, and he saw there something so murderous that he was for the moment startled.

It was an unnerving evening. Sanders was glad when his visitors had retired to his own room, which he had placed at their disposal. The real tragedy began next morning.

"I want every account book brought to this office," said the Major. "I want no explanations and no assistance. I am perhaps as good an auditor as the next man, Sanders—Mr. Sanders. What I should like, if it is possible, is for you to send away the gentleman who is affected—you were saying last night that you were due at a sort of palaver up the river. Perhaps you could take Mr. Tibbetts with you . . . ."

"How long will your audit take?" asked Sanders, in surprise.

"A week," said the other. "I want every voucher checked, and I'll check them myself. I don't wish to make charges against anybody, but my experience is that there's a deplorable amount of petty peculation going on unchecked."

"Are you suggesting that I am guilty of peculation?" asked Hamilton, who was present.

"Don't snap at me, sir," said the Major testily. "You have clerks, have you not? What is most likely to have happened is that, owing to a lack of efficient supervision, there may have been irregularities. I'll say no more than that."

Sanders was due at an important palaver; but, important as it was, it could have been postponed but for the Inspector-General's suggestion. He expressed his intention of leaving early the next morning, and that day was occupied in the collection of odd documents (many of which Bones found at the bottom of his trunks, and stored in odd crannies of his hut) and their arrangement in chronological order.

The Inspector-General was more amiable that night; told Sanders something about his wealth. He had large interests in oil fields in America, from which the bulk of his income was drawn. He had the finest house in Sussex—a show place, at which, to use his own words, "royalty had stayed."

The man was an arrant and vulgar snob. He made no disguise that he loathed Bones; never referred to him except as "that pup." He "travelled" a native clerk. Evidently from this man he had learned of the difficulties which the two sweating young officers had experienced in collecting their accounts together, and he gloated over their coming discomfiture.

Sanders welcomed the dawn that sent him, with Bones and half a dozen Houssas, to the *Zaire* and the clean morning air of the river.

At the appointed place he had an important territorial question to debate with five petty chiefs. He had also the problem of M'gala to settle; and, though he was not aware of it, this was the most important palaver of all.

There was a man of the Lower N'gombi whom nobody loved. Nor was it to be expected that any man should speak well of him or any woman look on him with a kind light in her eyes. For he was accurst from his birth by certain ghosts and devils, none of which was of itself of any great potency, though in the aggregate they had great power.

On the night M'gala came squalling into the world the witch doctor Tiki M'simba saw each and every devil creep into the mother's hut, and they did not come out again. There was a sceptical man once who pointed out the indisputable fact that Tiki M'simba had quarrelled with M'gala's father over a question of salt; but whether vengeance or clairvoyance was at the back of the doctor's vision, all the people of the Lower N'gombi accepted M'gala's misfortune. His mother hated him; his father, when he was still in the sprawling stage, left him on a sand spit, where crocodiles come in the heat of the day to bask.

The first crocodile and Mr. Commissioner Sanders appeared simultaneously. The rifle of Lieutenant Tibbetts deprived the crocodile of any interest in his projected meal, and Sanders brought the little black satiny thing aboard the *Zaire*, and held a palaver in the nearest village to discover its paternity. This discovery was simply made. M'gala's father came up for judgment.

"Lord, this child is full of devils," said that simple man, and related the circumstance of M'gala's birth.

It took an hour to tell, but the Commissioner was very patient.

"Bring me Tiki M'simba," he said at last, and the witch doctor came reluctantly. "O man," said Sanders, in his gentle way, which invariably heralded ungentle action, "you may see ghosts and devils and wonderful ju-jus, but none of these must do harm to any living man or woman."

"Lord," said Tiki M'simba, deceived by Sanders' courteous tone, "I see what I see."

"Also you shall feel what you feel," said Sanders.

They tied M'simba to a tree, and Abiboo, a sergeant of Houssas, whose right arm was diabolically strong, gave him twenty on the back for the good of his soul.

Little M'gala grew up, therefore, in an atmosphere of hostility. He never met M'simba in the village street but that seer did not fix him with a glare that terrified him. Little boys and girls, who played the queer games which little boys and girls play wherever they live, ostracized him. His father built him a small hut, which was the size of a dog kennel, and there he slept and had his meals. For very soon it was learned by ocular demonstration that M'gala brought bad luck.

If he looked at a goat for a long time, that goat died; if he stopped before a house to peer wistfully into its dark interior, some man or woman or child grew sick; if he spoke to any, they suffered pain. Once he watched a party of woodmen felling a tree. As he looked, the tree unexpectedly fell and killed two of them. The fishermen would not let him go on the river because he frightened the fish away.

He grew to youth, herring-ribbed, lank, silent, and, in his not unpleasant face, a curious intellectuality such as is not seen in native people. Nobody hindered him, for fear of Sanders. It was rumoured that neither poison nor axe could destroy him. Once, when he was fifteen, the exasperated elders of the village, stimulated by M'simba, hired a band of outcast people who lived on the edge of the N'gombi forest to carry him away, and do what they would. Four men went in search of him one day, when he was hunting in the forest. They were never again seen alive; their bodies, mangled by leopards, were found, but no leopards were seen, nor had any hunter found the spoor of one.

He built himself a hut away from his people and at the back of the settlement; and every day he came through the village, looking neither to the left nor to the right. Once he trod upon thorns, maliciously disposed in the path. He leaned against a hut while he cleared his feet of the thorns. A few paces further he was again wounded, and again he leaned on a hut while he pulled the thorns free.

That night those two huts were destroyed by fire, and nearly the whole of the village.

Tiki M'simba called a secret council of the oldest men, including the petty chief who was his creature.

"Sandi is now at the Rivers-meeting. One of us will go to him and tell him of all these terrible things. And we will ask him to take M'gala away, because of these happenings."

They chose a man whom Sanders liked, and he came to the junction of the rivers where the *Zaire* was moored, and in the evening Sanders gave him an audience and listened patiently to his complaint.

Now, Sanders treated all such matters as these with the greatest seriousness, for he knew how largely big events are determined by small causes, and so he did not grow impatient at talks of devils and ghosts, but considered them most profoundly, and even consulted Bones, who always assumed the gravity of a privy councillor deciding the issue of peace and war on such occasions.

"Very remarkable, dear old Excellency," he said, "but I have had cases similar. The superstitions of the indigenous native are remarkable. What about me going along and having a little chow about the law of averages? I could show these silly old blighters——"

"I don't think they want lecturing, they want relief. I will send for M'gala and take him to headquarters. He seems a very intelligent man, and I want a house boy."

"Lord," warned the messenger, "this man brings evil to all that he touches. Also he has threatened death to any who beat him. For no hand has been raised against him by your lordship's orders, also——"

"O ko!" said Sanders impatiently. "Let me see this wonder. A little beating does no man harm."

He was thinking at that moment of a certain Inspector-General.

M'gala left his village, and nobody came down to see him off, for fear of what might happen to those who watched his departure. It is a fact that he was hardly out of sight before three fat dogs, the property of Tiki M'simba, dropped dead for no reason whatever except perhaps heart disease engendered by over-feeding.

On its arrival Hamilton met the *Zaire* with a long face.

"There's the devil to pay," he said. "That swine has found both ledgers, and has openly accused me of doctoring the accounts. He says he'll break Bones, and is preparing a long report for Army Headquarters."

"What is the trouble?"

It was characteristic of Hamilton and the urgency of the crisis that he greeted Bones with a friendly smile.

"I'm afraid there's going to be hell, Bones," and told him what he had already told Sanders.

"Everything can be explained, dear old thing," said Bones airily. "If there are a few pounds out, I'll pay them out of my own pocket."

"To be exact," said Hamilton, "you're a hundred and sixty-three pounds out —I've never seen this brute so happy!"

The Major was indeed in a jovial frame of mind at breakfast. He rubbed his hands gleefully at the sight of Bones, and that misguided youth so misunderstood his geniality that he committed the heinous offence of slapping him on the back.

"Don't do that, sir, don't do it!" gasped Commeder Banks. "You are a fool, sir, and a criminal, sir——"

"And a cat burglar, dear old inspector," chortled Bones. "What about our going fishing—you and me and dear old Emmie?"

The girl cast an imploring look at him, but Bones was a notoriously bad reader of signs.

It took Sanders and Hamilton nearly an hour to bring to the young man a realization of the gravity of his position.

"Pull yourself together, Bones," said Hamilton gravely. "This may mean a court-martial. You remember he broke young Verney for exactly the same thing?"

Bones' face dropped.

"You don't mean he's serious, dear old boy? Why, I'm quite friendly with his wife!"

Hamilton groaned.

"You're not only friendly with his wife, but you've done every damned thing that you shouldn't do—he's after your blood and mine, too! He has been trying all the morning to get me to dissociate myself from you, and to swear that these accounts were entirely your affair."

All that morning the Major worked at his report. Before lunch he came out on to the verandah, dropped into an easy chair, and ordered a drink.

Sanders saw the new house boy come awkwardly on to the stoep, balancing a small tray and staring owlishly at the slopping glasses. He thought no more than that it was stupid of his cook to send this raw man; and then he heard a smack and saw M'gala go sprawling on to the floor, and the tinkle of breaking glass.

"Awkward beast!" roared the Inspector.

M'gala got up slowly. Never before had he been struck. His eyes were blazing and luminous. Then slowly he turned, and, walking down the steps, vanished round a corner of the building. The Inspector-General was wiping his trousers.

"That's an awkward devil you've got," he snarled.

"He's raw," said Sanders. "I only brought him down river this morning."

"I should jolly well say he was raw. Do you know what the brute did? He put his hand on my shoulder to steady himself when he was handing me the glass."

"Oh!" said Sanders blankly, and remembered the stories of M'gala that he had heard.

"I shall have to break that boy of yours, I'm afraid," the Major went on to a more pleasant topic. "I don't know how far you're responsible, but that is for the administrator to decide. His accounts are in a shocking state; there's a hundred and sixty-three pounds unaccounted for—Emmie, come here."

He called the girl sharply, and she sprang up from her chair, where she was sitting at the far end of the verandah, and almost ran to him. Sanders saw that she held something behind her.

"What was that letter you were reading?"

If it was possible, she turned even paler.

"There wasn't a mail in this morning?"

She shook her head.

"One you're treasuring, eh? Let me see it."

Even Sanders, sharp-eyed as he was, had not observed the girl's surreptitious reading.

"Let me see it."

Sanders saw the colour come into her face.

"I won't," she said, defiantly. "It is from a friend."

His lips curled in a grin.

"From Freddie?" he breathed.

"From Freddie," she said, and stood stiffly waiting for the storm.

Again that grimace of his.

"We'll talk about that after tiffin, shall we? Freddie—good God!"

He fumbled in his pocket for the key. And then, to his amazement, she snatched it from his hand and threw it across the rail of the stoep.

"You shan't do that, you shan't! Freddie means everything to me—everything! Now you know!"

She turned quickly and ran into the house, and the Inspector-General sat paralyzed with astonishment. Then he half rose from his seat, and fell back again.

"Good God!" he said, in an awed voice.

Sanders knew that for the first time in his life a woman had challenged his domination.

"That fellow Tibbetts . . . the man you call Bones . . . by God! He's been responsible . . . putting ideas into her damned head! What do you want?"

It was his native clerk. A telegram had come through. He snatched it from the man's hand, tore it open, and, fixing his pince-nez, read. Sanders saw his mouth open wider and wider, and into his pale blue eyes came a look of horror and bewilderment.

"What's this, what's this, what's this?" he muttered rapidly. "Hoax or something? Read that, Sanders—read it, my boy."

His voice was tremulous. Sanders took the sheet and read.

"Very urgent. Calder cables your oil shares dropped seven dollars fifty to seventy-five cents. Reported wells run dry. Panic in oil market. Shall I sell or hold?"

"All my money's in that!" wailed the man. "I'm ruined!"

Sanders said nothing. He saw the man reach mechanically for his topee, stagger down the steps and, crossing the square, disappear behind the Houssa lines. He had not returned by four. Sanders had an idea that he might have fallen into the river, and sent a search party for him.

They found him lying face down in the long, rank grass, a revolver gripped in his hand, and, near by, the dead body of M'gala. Nobody had heard the shot that killed the unlucky man. The spear he had thrust at Banks' throat was noiseless.

And that night, the white-faced wife sat in her bedroom, trying not to be thankful that the hand of M'gala the accurst had fallen upon her husband's shoulder.

THE END

www.ingramcontent.com/pod-product-compliance
Lightning Source LLC
Chambersburg PA
CBHW011517170626
46810CB00009B/3400

* 9 7 8 1 4 7 9 4 4 3 0 8 6 *